After they prayed and passed the food, Danny went on to describe the tall hero who had even attended hero school.

Ma's eyes widened. "Who is this man? We don't get many heroes coming through town." She looked at Danny. "Especially ones who went to hero school!"

The sudden memory of Derrick holding her in his arms warmed Allie's face. He was a stranger—and maybe it was the severity of her predicament—but she'd felt safe against his solid chest. *Stop it, Allie.*

She needed time to heal before allowing any man to bowl her over with his charm. Michael had practically abandoned her at the altar, and Luke...

There had to be a reasonable explanation for why her brother left them deep in debt. *Please, Lord.* Allie stabbed at a slice of onion, then met Ma's glance. "His name is Derrick Owens. He's a stranger in town on business."

"Well I'll be!" Ma's shrewd gaze hadn't missed Allie's emotions.

"I'm sure he's only here for a few days. We won't see him again."

"Hmm, you never know." Ma's smile lit her face, only to be outdone by Danny's.

Allie grimaced. "No matchmaking, you two."

CANDICE SPEARE lives in an old farmhouse in Maryland with Winston the African gray parrot and Jack the dog. You may contact her by visiting her Web site: www.candicemillerspeare.com.

NANCY TOBACK was born and raised in Manhattan and now resides in sunny Florida. Her passion for writing fiction began way back in grammar school. If there's spare time after being wife, mother, grandmother, writer, and avid reader, Nancy is a watercolorist and charcoal artist and enjoys gourmet cooking. You may e-mail her at backtonan@aol.com.

Don't miss out on any of our super romances. Write to us at the following address for information on our newest releases and club information.

Heartsong Presents Readers' Service
PO Box 721
Uhrichsville, OH 44683

Or visit www.heartsongpresents.com

A Hero for Her Heart

Candice Speare and Nancy Toback

Heartsong Presents

We'd like to acknowledge the following people who helped us: Bryon and Dawn Miller, who willingly answered any and all questions about Walla Walla, and John and Diana Blessing, who helped us with Washington facts.

If any of our readers wish to learn more about Walla Walla or things we've mentioned, here are some Web sites:

http://www.brightscandies.com/index.html

http://www.marcuswhitmanhotel.com/

http://wwvchamber.com/calendar.html

http://www.arbinifarms.com/

And last but never least, thank you, Wanda Dyson for the story.

A note from the Authors:
We love to hear from our readers! You may correspond with us by writing:

Candice Speare and Nancy Toback
Author Relations
PO Box 721
Uhrichsville, OH 44683

ISBN 978-1-60260-701-9

A HERO FOR HER HEART

Copyright © 2010 by Candice Speare and Nancy Toback. All rights reserved. Except for use in any review, the reproduction or utilization of this work in whole or in part in any form by any electronic, mechanical, or other means, now known or hereafter invented, is forbidden without the permission of Heartsong Presents, an imprint of Barbour Publishing, Inc., PO Box 721, Uhrichsville, Ohio 44683.

All scripture quotations are taken from the HOLY BIBLE, NEW INTERNATIONAL VERSION®. NIV®. Copyright © 1973, 1978, 1984 by International Bible Society. Used by permission of Zondervan. All rights reserved.

Our mission is to publish and distribute inspirational products offering exceptional value and biblical encouragement to the masses.

PRINTED IN THE U.S.A.

one

Sweat beaded on Allie's forehead as she adjusted her truck's air conditioner, but it didn't make a dent in the July heat. She headed onto a side street to avoid the Saturday morning crowds gathered for the parade to begin a series of events leading up to the Walla Walla Sweet Onion Festival scheduled for the following weekend.

"Excited?" She shot a glance at her eight-year-old nephew in the passenger seat. His black cotton T-shirt enhanced his bronze skin, and a familiar question crossed her mind. *What did his biological parents look like?*

"Yep." Smiling, Danny strained against the seat belt, dark eyes wide.

She winked at him, then backed her truck into a spot off the main drag. After she parked, she patted sweat off her brow and blew a damp piece of hair from her face. "Ready, Spiderman?"

Nodding, he unbuckled his seat belt. "We're going to Bright's before the parade, right?"

Allie leaned across the seat to kiss his forehead, but he backed away in mock horror. "Aunt Allie. I'm too old to be kissed in public."

"Oh, that's right." She sat back and sighed. "You're practically grown up. I'm sorry."

"That's okay," he said seriously. "But you need to try to remember."

"I'll try." Allie smiled. "Yes, we're going to Bright's. That's why I got us here before the parade starts."

The parade was the brainchild of Philip Maynard, mayor of Walla Walla and a member of the Walla Walla Valley Chamber of Commerce, whose close family owned nearby onion farms.

Although Philip wasn't a farmer himself—he owned a law firm—he wanted to ensure that people didn't forget the onion farmers. Whatever Philip's agenda, her nephew would enjoy the event.

Danny scrambled from the truck, slammed the door, and stood on the sidewalk waiting for her. She watched a car pass, then hopped to the ground and locked the doors. A fine layer of dust covered her red Chevy truck. With a sigh she ran her fingers over the white magnetic sign on the driver's door, wiping the dust off the black letters that spelled out VAHN'S FARRIER SERVICES—the business she'd learned from her father and shared with her brother Luke before he died.

"Come on, Aunt Allie. I'm hungry." Danny bounced from foot to foot.

"Bottomless pit," she joked as she walked around the truck to join her nephew. His appetite was enormous lately, digging into their already slim grocery budget, but she wouldn't complain. It was preferable to the months he'd refused to eat after his parents died.

She suddenly caught sight of Michael Maynard, the mayor's son, in his BMW, and she jumped back behind her truck, dragging Danny with her. What a coincidence that Michael was passing by just when she'd arrived. Or was it?

Danny tugged on her arm. "What's wrong?"

She put a finger to her lips. "Shh. I know I'm acting like a kid. But I'm hiding from someone."

"Who?" He stretched his neck around the truck. "Mr. Michael?"

"Yes." She yanked him back by the shirtsleeve. "And the whole point is to stay hidden."

"Why?" Danny sucked in his cheeks, narrowed his eyes, and studied her. That was Danny—sharp beyond his years. He crossed his arms. "I thought Michael was your friend."

Friend? Michael had been her fiancé until he'd cheated with another woman nine months ago. Now he wanted to date Allie again, which was out of the question. She would never be able to trust him, and fending off his advances got tiring.

She peered around the truck. Michael's car was gone. "Um, he is my friend, but I don't feel like talking to him today."

"Aunt Allie, that isn't right, is it? Can't I talk to him even if you don't?"

Allie bit her lip. She had good cause to avoid Michael, but no reason to drag the eight-year-old into the fray.

"You're right, Danny." Leave it to a kid to point out adult idiosyncrasies. "I might be twenty-eight, but no one said I was mature. Next time we see him, feel free to do whatever you'd like." She tucked a stray piece of Danny's black hair behind his ear. "Let's go. I want some of those mint truffles. And I know what you want."

"Gummi animals." They spoke simultaneously and laughed. Allie leaned down to kiss his dirt-smeared face, caught herself, and gave his hand a squeeze instead.

Above them wisps of marshmallow clouds scuttled across the blue sky, driven by hot wind. The sun bore down on her back as they headed for Bright's Candies.

"Hey, Allie!" Out of the side of her eye, she caught a glimpse of her friend Shannon a half block away waving her arms. Allie smiled. Who could miss her in a long denim skirt, tie-dyed, bell-sleeved blouse, and waist-length, blond braid?

"I've got our seats!" Shannon shouted. "Main and Second."

Nodding her understanding, Allie pointed in the direction of Bright's. Shannon gave a thumbs-up and disappeared into the crowd.

Allie smiled to herself. She loved Walla Walla with its rich history, old buildings, and forever friends.

Danny and Allie walked past the wrought-iron fence, which corralled tiny tables and chairs in front of Bright's windows. The gleaming glass door swung open without notice.

Allie slammed into a hard chest and gasped. A plastic bag landed on her feet, and jelly beans scattered around her sneakers.

She reeled back and looked up. If there were still such

things as pirates, the tall man in jeans and black polo shirt fit the bill, minus the eye patch. His black collar-length hair glinted blue in the summer sun. A razor-thin scar ran down his tanned face—from the top of his cheekbone to the corner of his mouth. His dark gaze latched onto hers.

Handsome, Allie admitted to herself.

The man looked down at Danny. He blinked, and his lips curved in a smile. Her perception of a pirate vanished. In its place was a man whose eyes emanated warmth. He suddenly turned his attention back to her.

"I'm sorry." Allie ripped her gaze from his and pointed at the sidewalk. "I made you drop your—"

"No problem." He stepped back and held the door open for them.

As she and Danny walked through the opening, she felt the man's eyes on them, but refused to turn around. She hadn't the time or desire for flirtation.

Allie placed her order at the counter while Danny moved toward Bright's chocolate city display, a massive concoction under glass made from chocolate and jelly beans. As she watched the perky teen behind the counter fill her requests, a voice from behind called her name. She recognized the distinctive baritone before she turned to see Philip Maynard's familiar and mostly bald head bobbing like a buoy amid the sea of waiting customers.

"I finally found you," he bellowed as he skirted others to reach her. The buttons on his short-sleeved dress shirt strained dangerously against his portly stomach. "I've got a blacksmith-type emergency."

An emergency. Of course. She just happened to be handy, which was why he didn't call his regular farrier.

"Hello, little man." Philip ruffled Danny's hair.

Danny wrinkled his nose and jabbed his finger in Allie's hip, an obvious attempt to remind her that this was *their* day.

Allie drew a deep breath, about to say, Thanks, but no thanks.

"I'll pay double your fee." Philip, always a sharp politician, had apparently read the hesitation on her face before she denied his request.

Double the fee? Yes, he probably knew she was strapped for cash. She had confided in his son, Michael-the-Cheat, and he must've relayed the info to his dad. Danny's adoptive parents, Luke and Cindy, had died with a will and a boatload of hidden debt against the business, which left her with guardianship and no money. Bottom line, she shouldn't turn down any job.

But. . . Allie pulled Danny closer. Today was different. She had no intention of working. "Sorry, Philip, but Danny and I are here to have fun."

"I know, I know, but the shoe on my Paige's horse is loose. She's part of this woman's club, and their group is riding in the parade in honor of the brave pioneer women who traveled the Oregon Trail—that was *my* idea." He paused, waiting for her appreciation.

Allie studied his red face. The Oregon Trail? Yes, that was a large part of local history, but this parade was supposed to be part of the onion festival. The connection between the two events eluded her, but she nodded anyway.

The mayor cleared his throat. "We can't have a spot missing from the formation." He dabbed his creased brow with a handkerchief. "Paige is on the verge of a meltdown."

Allie wasn't surprised. She'd known Paige, Michael's only sister, most of their lives. She was prone to emotional depths and heights that often left those around her dizzy. Even in a steady relationship with Allie's brother years ago, Paige had been a drama queen. And her hissy fits had only grown worse as she aged. How she'd ever gotten a law degree was beyond Allie's comprehension.

"Listen, Allie, all you have to do is hammer the shoe back on." Philip patted her arm. "I know you won't let us down."

Danny continued jabbing his finger into her hip. Allie gave him a warning glare and handed him his bag of gummi candy. That would keep his finger busy on something other than bruising.

Philip Maynard cleared his throat again. "Could mean more business for you, Allie."

Right. She recognized his words for what they were. An empty promise to use her services in the future.

Just hammer the shoe back on? Allie eyed Philip's hopeful face. Who knew why the shoe was loose? It could be bent. Or maybe the hoof had grown out. "You know, if I were your regular farrier, this wouldn't have happened." She always made it a point to know what her clients had planned for their horses, then ensured the animals were ready.

Philip's eyebrows twitched. "Could've sworn I told my secretary to give you a call." He wagged his head as if to blame the woman. "Why, just last week—"

"I'll do it." Allie saved him the embarrassment of expounding on his lie. Bills were stacking up. Danny's birthday was next week. The extra cash would be a blessing. Bottom line, she was in no position to refuse Philip's request.

Allie glanced down and offered Danny an apologetic smile, then looked at Philip's crimson face. "You want me to *hammer* the shoe back on the horse's hoof? What if I can't?"

"Why, I'm sure you can. You have your tools with you, right?" He dabbed again at the sweat running down his temples.

"Yes. In the truck. But if there's more wrong than just a missing nail, I won't be able to help you today."

Philip smiled. "Go get your tools, girl. I need you. Paige will have the horse at the market area at Main and Fourth." He whirled around, his portly body vibrating with tension as he pressed his way to the door.

"Aunt Allie, you promised." Danny's tone was whiny, and Allie felt a brief spurt of irritation, which she quickly squelched.

"I'm sorry, sweetie." She leaned close to his ear. "There's a reason I'm taking this job. A special event that's coming up. . ."

Danny's brow furrowed in concentration, then a big grin lit his face. "My birthday!"

"Yep." She high-fived him. "How about I get you settled with Shannon? That way you won't miss anything, and I'll be back as soon as possible."

Twenty minutes later, clad in her work chaps, Allie took the reins of a nervous chestnut gelding from Paige Maynard, who stood in a cloud of Chanel wearing a shorts outfit no doubt from the most expensive department store in the area.

"Daddy says this horse has good breeding. I don't care." She gave a one-shoulder shrug. "As long as he looks handsome riding in the parade."

"He's a beautiful animal." And a Thoroughbred, a breed used for horse racing and known for skittish nerves. Come to think of it, if Paige were a horse, this is exactly what she'd be like. White ringed his eyes, and his nostrils flared with his breaths. "What's his name?" Allie patted his muscled withers.

"Chester. He's. . ." Paige groaned and fanned her face, showing off a French manicure and a sparkling diamond bracelet. "My stomach hurts." Ever the drama queen, she rubbed her abdomen with jerky motions, and the horse tossed his head.

Allie positioned herself between Paige and Chester and began stroking his neck. How lucky she was that Paige had never gotten her way and married Luke.

Paige continued to fidget behind her. "Where's Danny?"

"He's with Shannon." Allie willed herself to be patient. Was God okay with her praying for Paige to disappear?

"How is the little guy?" Either Paige had been miraculously healed of her ailment or didn't have stomach pains to begin with.

"You mean Danny?" Allie kept her focus on the horse. For some odd reason, she was reluctant to discuss her nephew with Paige even though she'd handled his adoption for Luke and Cindy.

"Yes. Is he recovering? I mean, it's got to be hard, losing both his parents and all. Especially Luke."

Allie flashed a glance over her shoulder at Paige. Her tears at Luke's funeral had been more than show. She'd never gotten over her high school crush on him. "Danny's not so little anymore. And he's doing well, thanks. I had him in grief counseling. . . ." She felt like a mare, protecting her foal. "I'm thinking of adopting Danny."

Paige pressed her hand to her chest. "Adopting him?"

"Sure, why not?" Allie smiled. "It'll make Danny feel more secure."

"But you're already his legal guardian, right? Why go through the courts to—"

"Yep, I'm Danny's legal guardian." She fought hard to keep pride out of her tone. "But I think adopting him might make him feel more secure."

"I'm. . ." Paige took a deep breath and rubbed her stomach again. "I'm feeling queasy. I'm scared I might have heatstroke or something."

"You should go get a drink of cold water." Allie willed Paige to leave. She'd then be able to calm Chester without interference.

"Yes, I suppose you're right. Besides, I need to change into my costume. I'll be back."

Was that a promise or a threat? Allie listened to Paige's footsteps recede, then turned her full attention to the horse.

"You know, big guy," she whispered, "with an owner like that, it's no wonder you're jittery. She makes me jittery, too."

The white rings around his eyes slowly disappeared. She stroked his neck, and he whickered softly.

"Okay, fellow. I think you're ready. Let's do this." She pulled her tools near, lifted his hoof, and placed it between her legs. She'd appreciate her hoof stand, but hadn't felt like carrying it or bringing her truck with all her equipment to check a single shoe. Sure enough, there were nails missing. Fortunately, the hoof was fine, and the shoe wasn't bent. She'd be able to make the repair.

She picked up several nails, placing them between her lips, then grabbed the hammer. After driving in the nail, she bent it back, and set the next one in place.

A shadow fell over her, and she glanced up into the coal black eyes of the tall pirate she'd run into earlier.

two

Allie's face heated. She dropped Chester's hoof and rose, hammer in hand.

He flashed a beautiful smile. "So we meet again."

The man made her feel discombobulated, something she rarely experienced. Allie found herself searching for a clever response. "Sorry I bashed into you earlier. I hope you didn't lose too many of your jelly beans."

He held up a bag of candy. "No, I still have some." His gaze swept her and Chester. "You're a blacksmith."

"Farrier. And I'm glad it's obvious. I'd hate to think I'm doing this with no experience." She smiled and realized she was flirting, so she toned it down. "I guess I could also be considered a blacksmith, but I don't do a lot of the heavier forging of iron or steel objects. I just shoe horses."

His smiled broadened, and his black eyes snapped with the kind of interest that flattered her. "I'm Derrick Owens. I'm in town for business."

"Allie Vahn." She gave him a quick full-body glance. His jeans and polo shirt looked expensive. In fact, his persona screamed toned and well-to-do, which brought her back to reality. She'd had enough of spoiled men with a sense of entitlement like Michael.

The horse jerked his head, and she chided herself for allowing her attention to wander.

"I need to get back to work here." Allie gestured at Chester.

"Definitely a pleasure to meet you again." He nodded, gave her another hundred-watt smile, then sauntered away.

"I know where the term *butterflies in my stomach* comes from," she murmured as she turned her concentration back to the shoe and drove in the last nail. Finally finished, she

13

stood, stretched, and began to remove her chaps.

Philip Maynard appeared as if on cue. "You done there?" He thrust out his chest like a banty rooster. "We don't have long now before—"

"I'm done." Allie set her tools on the ground and un-snapped the leg straps of her leather chaps. "I'll mail you a bill." She skimmed the crowd with a detached air. The dark-haired stranger was nowhere in sight—and she had no good reason to feel disappointed. She did not need another man to deal with right now.

"I'll get Paige." With labored breaths, Philip ambled away.

"Whatever." The horse shuffled nervously. Philip's presence had disturbed him. Allie rubbed Chester in a soothing gesture. How had a simple day at the parade become so complicated? She had to get back to Danny.

She rested her head against Chester's warm neck, breathing in the distinct pleasant odor of horse. "C'mon, Mayor, I've got to get going."

"Allie." Philip must have heard her thoughts. He was barreling toward her, waving frantically.

The horse twitched. Allie straightened and watched, open-mouthed. How could Philip move so fast? What a red-faced, sweaty mess to behold.

"We've got a huge problem," he gasped when he reached her.

Paige wasn't the only one on the verge of heatstroke. Allie stepped back and attempted to hand the horse's reins to him, but he shook his head, shooing her away. "I don't know what to do."

Allie's stomach clenched. The look in his eyes told her his problem was about to become hers. "Do about what?" Her tone was snarly, but she wasn't about to apologize.

"Paige has worked herself into a fit. She's sick to her stomach."

"And?" The desperation in his eyes didn't move her. "Someone can just fill in for her, can't they?"

His eyebrows shot up, and he smiled. "Why, that's brilliant.

You can do it."

"Oh no." She shoved the reins at him. "No way. I'm here to watch the parade with Danny. Besides, I don't have a costume."

Philip Maynard's slit-eyed perusal told her he was calculating the best way to get her to acquiesce. "How about I pay you *three* times your rate for hammering on that shoe? And you can wear Paige's costume. You're about the same size."

Allie opened her mouth to say no, but the cost of Danny's party and the mounting bills with late fees made her hold her tongue. Danny might enjoy seeing her ride in the parade, she reasoned. Or maybe not.

"I'll do it under one condition." She couldn't believe her own words.

Philip breathed hard, watching her as if he was afraid of what she was going to ask.

"You write me a check for that amount and give it to me today."

He nodded heartily. "You got it."

She handed him Chester's reins. "I'll meet you back here shortly. I need to explain to Danny what's going on."

The mayor smiled. "I'll have someone bring you Paige's costume. Tell me where you'll be."

She did while mentally chiding herself for not bartering for more money. Finally, she turned to the horse, who tossed his head and shuffled uneasily. "Get over yourself, Chester. We're about to become even better acquainted."

❧

The sun warmed his skin as Derrick strode down Main Street toward his next goal. Walla Walla was a charming town. He'd been here on business before, but had never walked the streets. The parade, which he hadn't intended to watch, would start soon. He was drawn by the simplicity of it all. When was the last time he'd seen a parade? He couldn't remember. Today he'd intended to go for a drive and scour the outskirts of town for land that had potential for developers, then he'd contact the owners and see if they were interested in selling—a partial ruse. He groaned. He had a client interested in developing property, but land acquisition wasn't Derrick's actual purpose for coming to Walla Walla, and he was having trouble staying on task.

Derrick reached into his bag of jelly beans and popped one into his mouth. He'd lost some of the candy running into the petite auburn in front Bright's, but the loss was well worth it if his hunch was right.

Allie. A farrier? He smiled at the memory of her holding the hoof of the large horse. Tiny as she was, she likely had a magic touch with the animals in order to do her job effectively.

Derrick rested his back against the rough bark of a tree and dug into his bag of candy. Allie had special eyes—green and expressive. She was different from any woman he'd ever met—in what way, he couldn't exactly say. She had shown a flash of interest in him, too. He'd grown accustomed to that kind of attention from women and had used it to his advantage in the past. But Allie's interest had died as quickly as it had come. The old Derrick would have turned on the charm to engage her again, but the new Derrick lost the desire to lead women on. Besides, he wasn't here to find a girlfriend. He was here to get information and return to his own life and home.

Could his search be over already? If God was on his side, Allie and the boy held the answers he needed.

Derrick stuffed the last of the candies into his mouth and tossed the bag into a nearby trash receptacle. His cell phone rang, and he quickly snatched it from the holder on his belt, glanced at the number on the screen, and flipped it open.

"Hello, Dad." Derrick spoke around the chewy candy that threatened to glue his jaw shut. He could practically see his father holding a pen over the leather-bound planner on his desk opened to his to-do list. Now his father could put a line through "Call Derrick."

"Just checking in, son. Have you found any potential properties?"

"Not yet. I'll keep hunting over the next day or so. Today the town is caught up in this onion festival parade. It's rather charming the way—"

"Please keep me posted." Dad harumphed. "I'm glad you're taking the initiative to find more business for Owens Realty."

Guilt rattled Derrick. His interest in land in Walla Walla gave him a legitimate excuse to be in town, but truth be told, finding property wasn't his priority. He tapped his fingers against his thigh. Did the omission of certain information constitute a lie? Possibly. And untruths, whether white lies, outright lies, or stretching the truth, had a way of coming home to roost.

"Your mom said to tell you"—Dad cleared his throat— "that Sandy. . .er. . .Sandy is eating well."

A euphemism that meant Derrick's sister was having a good day and her will to live had given her temporary victory over the lymphoma that was killing her. Their father would not show his emotion, nor would he concede that his daughter was going to die.

"Good," Derrick said, blinking back sudden tears. Sandy had little time left. He needed to find what he was looking for here. For her sake. He'd do anything for his sister.

After he signed off with his father, Derrick dialed Sandy's cell.

"Derrick." Her voice was stronger than he'd heard it in a while. "Have you got news?"

He stopped pacing and made way for a group of rowdy teens. "I think I do."

"Really? Already? I prepared myself to accept this was a wild-goose chase."

What if he was wrong? Last thing he wanted was to get her hopes up, only to squash them. "Today, just by chance, I ran into a boy who could be the one we're looking for, but I can't promise yet."

"Wow. How do you know he's my son if you just ran into him?"

"The family name is Vahn," Derrick said. "Granted, they might not be the Vahns who adopted your son, but he's got our eye and hair color."

"Oh, Derrick, that would be an answer to prayer." Sandy's strained breathing made him short of breath. "Remember, I don't want them to know who you are or who I am. I just want to be sure my son's happy with the people who adopted him, okay? Promise me."

Derrick was silent.

"I said you have to promise me."

"Yes, fine." Derrick kicked his booted foot against the hydrant. "I won't let on."

"Thank you." Sandy sighed. "How can you forgive me, D-man? Giving away my baby and not telling anyone?"

"I didn't let on how shocked I was at first. I was afraid my reaction would send you into a decline."

She laughed. "I'm already declining."

A hard knot formed in his throat. "That's not funny, Sandy."

"I think my prognosis gives me the right to laugh at whatever I please."

Derrick had to smile. His sister's humor in the face of death amazed him. "You were desperate, Sandy. Not in your right mind at the time you signed away your baby."

"That's putting it mildly." She laughed softly. "More like a drug-induced alternate reality."

"I know. I feel guilty because I didn't come and rescue you back then."

"I wouldn't have let you. Believe me." She paused. "It's funny how coming to the Lord changes your perspective, isn't it? You look at life so differently. The things that used to be important aren't."

"True." Derrick nodded, but sometimes he worried the process of sanctification was taking too long in his own life. "You gave me all the info you had, right? That's just the names of the parties involved and this one picture."

"Yes. It was a closed, private adoption. I signed a bunch

of papers. I was given the picture of my son and his birth parents, but nothing more. I promised the lawyer, Paige, that I'd never attempt to contact the parents. It all happened right after he was born, and I was in a fog—worse than normal." Her voice grew raspy. "Knowing what I do now, I think they gave me more money than they should have. Of course, I promptly squandered it on drugs. It's been almost nine years, and the first three of those are like a nightmare sequence. . . . I can't even remember everywhere I lived up until I returned home." Her voice had weakened during their conversation. "D-man. . .I don't think I have much time left."

"I won't let you down, sis." Derrick released a jagged breath. "You take care, okay?"

"I will. And I'm praying God will guide you in the direction you need to go. I'm just so glad this all worked out the way it did with you having business in Walla Walla."

Derrick swallowed hard and severed their connection. He couldn't even be totally truthful with his sister. Would his newly found Savior bless his overall efforts, despite what he had to do to get there?

God, please forgive me.

❧

Allie sat in formation with the women's club members. A hot, brisk breeze blew against her face and moved the skirts of her pioneer costume. She felt baked in the sun. A good thing she'd remembered to slather on sunscreen this morning. The leader of the group told her they'd be riding in a perfect diamond formation, with Allie at the back point of the diamond and the rest of the group in front of her.

The parade began, led by the local VFW. Behind that was a float ordered by Philip to be built by the historical society, complete with a papier-mâché replica of an onion and a huge banner bearing the town's name. Several members of the historical society were on board, dressed in overalls and jeans, holding garden tools. The mayor trailed in a blue convertible, followed by two cars filled with town dignitaries.

Although Chester walked quietly, she sensed the Thoroughbred's tension. Allie relaxed her position, heels down, back straight, hands resting lightly on the saddle horn.

From the side of her eye, she thought she caught a glimpse of Derrick, the pirate. Then the folks on the float in front of her brought out a banner. As it unfurled, Chester danced a few nervous steps. She leaned and spoke to him gently while stroking his neck.

The banner snapped in the wind, the white material undulating like a wave of water. Chester reared, eyes wide with fright. The women gave her wide berth. The leader of the group was hollering, which only added to Chester's discomfort.

Heart beating wildly, Allie fought to control the horse. She finally got all four hooves back on the pavement and took a breath.

The banner snapped again, and the panicked animal squealed.

"Chester!" Allie screamed. His hooves slid on the pavement. He was about to fall. She loosened the reins. Chester reared, ears back, eyes rimmed white.

Allie weighed her options while Chester snorted and danced. She could ride the crazy Thoroughbred through the streets of Walla Walla until he threw her or slipped on the pavement and fell, possibly crushing her. Or she could try to jump from his back now, risking broken bones or—

Chester's muscles tensed.

Allie released her feet from the stirrups and prepared to leap.

three

With no time to think, Derrick snatched the tiny farrier from the horse by her waist. She was heavier than she appeared, and her long dress wrapped around his legs, making it difficult to walk. As he carried her away from the horse, Allie squeezed his neck in a viselike grip. He held her closer and longer than necessary, guilty for liking the feel of her next to him.

Allie's grasp tightened, and the subsequent lack of air to his lungs quickly diminished his pleasure. He set her feet on the sidewalk, then peeled her arms from around his neck.

"You're okay now," he said, massaging his windpipe. "You can relax."

Her eyes jerked open, and she stared at him. "You!"

He pointed to himself. "Me?"

With her breathing still rapid and her face white, she continued to stare at him. He checked to see if he had a piece of a jelly bean stuck in his front teeth. After a long pause, she appeared to collect her composure, though her face remained ashen and her hands shook. "Sorry. I owe you a huge thanks."

Derrick nodded, then assured the bystanders she was okay.

Allie scanned the streets, wide-eyed. "Where is Chester. . . the horse?" she asked. "That Philip Maynard—what was he thinking, putting that animal in this parade? Poor thing."

Derrick made a quick mental note about the name *Maynard*, then put his hand on the small of her back and moved her away from the road. "The 'poor thing' took off around the float, but some people up ahead caught him. And it appears the parade is moving on without you."

"Good." Her gaze raked the crowd. "I've got to find my nephew. I hope he isn't worried." She brushed past him and headed for Second Avenue.

Derrick followed her. They didn't go far before he caught sight of the boy who spotted Allie and grinned widely.

"Aunt Allie!" He ran to her, slamming into her legs. Only Derrick's quick grasp of her shoulders kept her from falling backward. When she regained her balance, he released her.

"Aunt Allie, you were like a rodeo rider! Wow!"

She smiled and pulled him close. "I'll probably feel like a rodeo rider tomorrow. All bruised and battered."

Derrick glanced from Allie to Danny, whose black eyes looked so much like his own. Aunt and nephew. Where were his parents?

"You guys. . ." A blond walked up to them, denim skirt swirling around her ankles. She carried a large black bag, which she set next to Allie. "Your tools, Ms. Farrier." Then she looked over Allie's shoulder. "I'd say you're a hero, mister."

Derrick shook his head, about to protest, but Allie turned and faced him. "Without you my landing would have been awfully hard. I might have even broken a few bones."

"All in a hero's day's work."

Allie laughed and motioned toward the blond. "This is my friend, Shannon O'Brien. Shannon, this is Derrick. . ." She frowned. "Owen?"

"Derrick *Owens*," he said, acknowledging Shannon. He dropped his gaze to Danny, who had been staring at him with a wrinkled forehead.

The boy traced an invisible line down his own face, perfectly matching the placement of Derrick's scar. "Did you get hurt bad?"

Allie offered an apologetic smile. "Danny honey, it's not polite to make comments like that."

"It's okay." Derrick pointed to his cheek. "I got hurt a long time ago. It's a scar. Do you have any scars?"

The boy nodded. "On my leg. I fell out of a tree. I was pretending to be Spiderman."

"So I'm not the only hero around here then."

Danny shrugged. "I'm a hero when I wear my Spiderman costume, I guess."

Derrick laughed. Could this be his sister's boy?

Shannon reached over and hugged Allie. "I certainly hope old man Maynard paid you well for your services. He owes you after that ride."

Old man Maynard? Derrick's heart thumped. There was that name again.

"Yes, he's going to pay me *very* well." Allie tilted her chin. "We're going to have a real shindig for Danny's birthday."

"Good. You probably deserve twice what he's giving you." Shannon's gaze snapped to Derrick again. "You're a real, live hero, Derrick Owens, and they're in short supply around here. You new in town?"

A hero? If they knew why he was here, they might not think so. Derrick masked his discomfort with a smile. "I'm checking out a few opportunities in the area for the contracting company I work for."

Shannon's eyes lit up. "Are you looking to buy land? Allie might be selling her land."

"Really?" He glanced at Allie.

"Not a for-sure thing." Her smile had faded, and she was frowning at her friend.

Shannon patted Allie's arm. "Just remember that God opens doors when you least expect it." She stepped back. "Well, I'll let Allie explain if she wants to. I need to scoot. I have to get back to my shop to relieve my temporary help."

"Thanks for watching Danny," Allie called after her.

"Anytime. I'll see you after dinner tonight." Shannon waved over her shoulder and swirled away in her flowing denim skirt.

Allie took a breath as if she was going to say something, but before she could speak, an overweight man, red in the face, trundled down the sidewalk at a clip that surprised Derrick given his size.

"Allie!" His chest heaved with his breaths. "Are you okay?

I thought you were going to get killed."

Allie scowled. "And I'd have *you* to thank for it, Mayor."

He sputtered for a moment. "The horse was a little temperamental, but we thought he'd be fine. We just got him, you know."

"Gee, now you tell me." Irritation sparked in Allie's green eyes.

Derrick observed the shade of the mayor's face and hoped he wasn't going to have to perform CPR.

"You okay? Danny okay? This isn't going to affect him, is it? I mean, I wouldn't want things to get worse for him, poor little man."

Allie's body went rigid, and the sparks in her eyes turned to fire. "Some things are best left unsaid, aren't they?"

The mayor flushed, glancing from her to the boy and back again. "Yes, well. . .do you need a doctor?" He drew a noisy breath. "Do you have, er, insurance?"

Derrick watched the exchange with interest. What things were best left unsaid?

"No worries, Mayor. I'll be fine. But we need to get going." She held out her hand.

He fumbled in his shirt pocket and pulled out a check. "Ink isn't even dry on this. Here you go." He nodded at Derrick, then turned and dashed off.

Allie's narrowed gaze followed him for a minute, then she opened the check and smiled. "Ha, five times my going rate is almost worth taking that wild pony ride."

"Is that a lot of money?" Danny asked. "Does that mean you and Granny can buy me that handheld game system?"

"Possibly, but only if you don't nag me." Allie stared fondly at her nephew.

"Birthday boy?" Derrick asked, taking mental notes.

Danny grinned. "My birthday is next Saturday. Aunt Allie and Granny are giving me a party. Now I might get better presents."

Allie thumped his head with her finger. "That's enough

about presents, Spiderman."

Danny nodded, but his eyes still shone.

Derrick's breaths came more quickly. Could it be this easy?

"Shannon is right." Allie interrupted his thoughts. She refolded the check and held it tightly in her hands, then looked Derrick squarely in the eyes. "You are a hero."

Hero? "Could be because you've known me less than fifteen minutes."

Danny hopped from one foot to the other. "That was cool, the way you caught Aunt Allie. Where did you learn to do that?"

The force of the boy's enthusiasm was irresistible. Pretending solemnity, Derrick glanced around as if to make sure the coast was clear, then leaned down and whispered, "I learned it in hero school."

Danny's eyes widened. "Is that where your face got hurt?"

"No, but it does make me look more heroic. I graduated at the top of my class." He straightened and glanced at Allie. "And because I'm a hero, I insist I walk you to wherever you're going while I carry your tools."

"You don't need to do that," she said quickly.

"Oh, but I do." He lifted his eyes to the summer sky and scratched his chin as though he were thinking hard. "See, it's rule number. . .um. . .twenty-one, I think. 'After saving a damsel in distress, always see her safely home or to her vehicle, whichever applies.'" He crossed his arms. "I scored a perfect hundred on that test. Of course, I stayed up all night cramming. And it's been awhile."

Allie's lips twitched. "How does one study for a *hero test*?"

Derrick placed his hand on his chest as though making a pledge. "Sorry, I can't reveal the secrets of a hero. It's in the rules. Number one, and I quote, 'No method, secret, rule, or procedure shall be revealed to anyone at any time.'" He paused and winked again at Danny. "And number two says, 'No hero will ever be caught bragging on exploits, whether his own or those of a fellow hero.'"

·The boy's wide smile brought cheer to his heart, but it was Allie's grin that made his insides warm. He'd have to be careful. Old flirting habits died hard, and he couldn't afford the complication of an attraction. He had information to gather, then he'd be gone. Most of all, she could never know why he was here.

"All right, Derrick Owens, hero extraordinaire," Allie said, unaware of his turmoil, "you may walk us to my truck."

Derrick fought another surge of guilt. He leaned over to pick up Allie's tools so she wouldn't see his eyes. As he did someone called her name, and he glanced up. A tall, slender man in creased jeans and a brand-name polo shirt was jogging toward them.

"It's Mr. Michael," Danny said in a stage whisper, glancing up at Allie.

"So it is." Her face was an interesting study in consternation. "Go ahead, Danny."

"Hi!" he said to the blond man.

"Danny, good to see you." He gave the boy a quick brush on his head, then stopped close to Allie and touched her arm possessively. "My father just told me what happened. Are you all right?"

The mayor's son. Derrick recognized the resemblance now. Both had the same classic Roman nose. He also recognized disappointment in Danny's eyes. Perhaps he hadn't gotten the response he'd expected from *Mr. Michael*.

"I'm okay." Allie shrugged. "Just stiff and tired."

Pointing at Derrick, Danny said, "He rescued Aunt Allie."

Michael frowned and shook his head. "I can't believe my father would allow anyone to ride that horse. If it had been Paige, she might have been killed. She's not nearly as good a horseman as you."

Paige? Derrick's shoulders went rigid. *Lord, You are answering Sandy's prayers.*

"Why your father would allow your sister to even be near that horse is beyond me," Allie said. "Two nervous Nellies."

"Well, we owe you. How about I take you home?"

Allie straightened her narrow shoulders. "I'm just fine, Michael." She sidestepped him and snatched Danny's hand. "Derrick is walking us to my truck."

Michael turned to him, a flash of surprise in his eyes. . .and irritation. He extended his hand. "I don't believe I've had the pleasure."

The man didn't look like he was feeling pleasure. Derrick clasped his hand. "Derrick Owens."

"Michael Maynard." The guy stared at him with intense curiosity. "You aren't from around here."

"No, I'm from the Tri-Cities. I'm here on business."

"I've got to get going. We're hungry," Allie said, cutting off their conversation.

"I'll call you later then." Michael glanced from Allie to Derrick and nodded.

Allie didn't respond. She squeezed Danny's shoulder with her right hand and began to walk away, pulling him along. Derrick had no choice but to follow.

As he followed, her tools in tow, Derrick felt Michael's eyes on his back and fought the temptation to turn and look at him. He hurried to catch up with Allie, whose strides were long and fast for such a petite woman.

Could he have imagined Michael Maynard's possessive attitude toward Allie? Not likely. Maybe they were dating. Derrick loosened his tight grip on her tool case. None of his business if the two were involved. With Sandy dying, he had to find answers quickly. He breathed a prayer of thanks to the Lord for blessing his efforts so far. He'd been in Walla Walla less than two days, and he was confident he'd found his nephew. He needed a bit more information—then he'd hightail it out of this town.

four

As they prepared for dinner after the parade, Allie laughed when Danny described the wild horse incident to his grandmother while she sliced ham at the kitchen counter.

"I could have been killed!" Allie feigned a scowl.

"Not you, Aunt Allie. You ride too good."

"Too well," Allie corrected. She popped two painkillers into her mouth, took a drink of water, sat, and stifled a groan. Stiffness had already set in.

Her mother chuckled. "I'm not surprised you're okay. You always were good with horses. And you were such a tomboy. So independent. That's your father's fault."

"You know you did just as much to encourage me."

Ma hid a smile and shook her head. She carried a platter of cold ham along with a bowl of onion, cucumber, and tomato salad to the dinner table. "Ah, the perfect summer meal." Allie's mouth watered.

After they prayed and passed the food, Danny went on to describe the tall hero who had even attended hero school.

Ma's eyes widened. "Who is this man? We don't get many heroes coming through town." She looked at Danny. "Especially ones who went to hero school!"

The sudden memory of Derrick holding her in his arms warmed Allie's face. He was a stranger—and maybe it was the severity of her predicament—but she'd felt safe against his solid chest. *Stop it, Allie.*

She needed time to heal before allowing any man to bowl her over with his charm. Michael had practically abandoned her at the altar, and Luke. . .

There had to be a reasonable explanation for why her brother left them deep in debt. *Please, Lord.* Allie stabbed at a slice of onion, then met Ma's glance. "His name is Derrick Owens. He's a stranger in town on business."

"Well I'll be!" Ma's shrewd gaze hadn't missed Allie's emotions.

"I'm sure he's only here for a few days. We won't see him again."

"Hmm, you never know." Ma's smile lit her face, only to be outdone by Danny's.

Allie grimaced. "No matchmaking, you two. Don't think I haven't overheard you talking about finding me a man after Michael and I split up. And this one? A total stranger? He could be an ax murderer for all we know."

"What a mind you have." Ma clucked her tongue.

"He's not an ax murderer," Danny said as he chewed his food. "He's a hero."

Allie wagged her finger at him. "Don't talk with your mouth full."

The two conspirators said nothing else, but their exchanged glance spoke volumes. Allie determined to forget the whole topic—and the *hero*—and enjoy her meal. She brought a forkful of salad to her lips when her cell phone started to vibrate, dancing on the table next to her plate. She glanced at the screen, held back a snort, and continued to eat.

"You going to answer that?" Ma asked.

"It's Michael." Allie forced a smile for Danny's sake. "And we're busy eating dinner."

Ma dismissed the phone with a wave. "Right, let's eat." She understood how badly Michael had hurt her. "I have some good news."

"Oh?" Allie salted her food. "Do tell."

"I'm going to work for Shannon."

Allie's fork hit her plate. "What?"

"She's thinking about expanding by adding a shop in the Tri-Cities. She'll need someone to manage her store here. I'm going to start part-time."

"Shannon's really going through with that?" Allie's appetite fled. Her best friend. . .leaving. "I knew she was mulling it over, but—"

"Seems she believes the Lord is leading her there, and she'll be closer to where her parents live."

"Miss Shannon's leaving?" Danny's eyes grew watery.

Allie could've given herself a swift kick for elaborating in front of her nephew. Danny had suffered enough loss. "Don't worry. The Tri-Cities are only an hour from Walla Walla."

"Right," Ma assured.

"Ma, you've already got a job cleaning the church." Allie shook her head. "No. I don't approve." As soon as the words left her mouth, she regretted them. A combination of the stressful day, a stiff body, annoyance at Michael, and worry about the future made her snippy.

Ma sat back in her chair and crossed her arms. "Young lady, I don't think you should be telling your mother what to do. And two part-time jobs equal full-time pay."

"I'm sorry." Chastised, Allie took a deep breath. "But I don't want you working so hard. At your age you should be looking forward to some time off."

Ma's blond brows nearly hit her hairline. "Are you insinuating I'm old?"

Danny's head swiveled back and forth between the two like he was watching a tennis match.

"Not at all. You're not old. In fact, if we looked anything alike, we could be sisters. But. . .we should talk later," Allie said with a slight dip of her head in Danny's direction.

"Yes, we should." Ma's eyebrows were drawn into a frown. "And we will."

Allie barely tasted the remainder of her meal. The minute dinner was over she stood and gathered plates.

"Stop." Ma stayed her hand. "Danny and I will clean up. You sit and rest and give those painkillers time to work. I watched you limp into the kitchen earlier."

Allie sighed. She couldn't deny that every muscle in her body ached. Regular exercise and her job kept her fit, but she hadn't the time lately to do much riding. Clinging to Chester with all her strength during his rampage at the parade left her sore in places she didn't realize she had muscles. "All right, thanks."

Danny popped out of his seat and took the plates she'd gathered. Allie shifted in her chair, trying to find a position that didn't hurt. She longed to lie down, but she had a date with Shannon tonight at which time she'd lecture her friend about offering Ma a job without first consulting her. Not to mention reminding Shannon that Allie didn't want Shannon to move away. What would she do without her best friend close by?

Allie looked at her mom and mentally rehearsed ways to get her to understand she didn't need a second job. When Danny had finished cleaning the table, Allie crooked her finger at him, and he came over and stood in front of her.

"Spiderman, why don't you go feed the horses."

He grinned. "You want to talk to Granny without me, don't you?"

She squeezed his hands and smiled. "You're too smart by far."

He tapped his head with his index finger, then skipped out the back door.

Allie rested her weary head against her fisted hand. "Ma, I can support all of us."

"No, you can't." Ma shut the dishwasher and began rinsing the sink. "We aren't making it, Allie. You know that as well as I do. You work so hard, honey, but you've lost business because you can't keep up the workload you and Luke maintained together. This property is too big. The place wasn't meant for two women alone."

The words cut deep. First Daddy died, a year later Luke, then the dissolution of her engagement to Michael. No adult men in their household. No heroes to save their property. "Maybe we won't have to sell. We can lease out more land."

"Not fast enough to catch up with the bills."

"Okay then, we sell off land like we talked about. Then we could pay off debt."

"Do you know how long that would take?" Ma shook her head. "We have bills due now. We don't have months to wait."

"It's not fair. Not to you, not to Danny. None of it is fair."

Ma crossed the kitchen, sat across from her, and took her hands. "You know what I'm going to say."

"Yes, I do." Allie snatched her hands from under her mom's. "What you always say. God never promised life would be fair. Just that He'd walk through the trials with us. You've said it a million times, but—"

"It's true. Nowhere in the Bible does God promise us a bed of roses."

"More like a bunch of thorns." Allie clenched her fists.

"Honey, I know you're still angry about a lot of things. Your daddy dying. Luke and Cindy's accident, and Luke leaving so much debt. You being unable to pull in the kind of money you want to—"

"Of course I'm angry. Especially at what Luke did." Allie bit her lip. Why hurl bitterness at her mother?

"Yes, I know. He misrepresented some things."

Allie slapped her palm on the table. "*Misrepresented things?* He got credit cards for our business without my knowledge. He kept a second set of books to cover the debts. And he had the bills sent to a PO box. That's worse than misrepresentation. He was living a lie."

"You're right. But you don't know why he did it."

"No. Neither do you." Allie glared at her mother. "That's even worse. I've been lied to by two men I loved more than anyone else in the world. The latest being Michael the Cheater."

"What Michael did to you was awful. I won't defend him."

"At least we agree on that." Allie groaned. "There is no good reason to lie. No excuse for it."

"I agree with you in principle, but we can't stand in judgment of someone else." Ma sighed. "Luke was my son as well as your brother. Don't you think I have questions, too?

But I have to forgive him."

"I loved him so much," Allie said. "Looked up to him." Beyond what she could express in words. She'd had this discussion with her mom too many times. Exhaustion washed over her, and Allie got to her feet, ready to escape to the quiet of her bedroom.

"It's like you're trying to make up for Michael's transgressions and Luke's by being perfect." Ma tapped her finger on the table to emphasize her words. "You want to rescue Danny and me by yourself, and that's admirable, Allie, but you can't. Your stubbornness is not going to pay the bills. You have to learn to be humble. To ask for help. From me and from others. I'm ready to go to the pastor to get his advice."

Allie swiped angrily at the tears in her eyes. "I don't want people to know."

"I understand, I really do. But if we lose everything, they'll find out, and then we'll look foolish. I've been trying to tolerate your obstinacy, but I'm not going to let us go under."

The firm set of Ma's chin told her she was losing the battle, and she fought tears.

"How about a change of topic?" Ma, ever the peacemaker, smiled. "Remember that tomorrow Danny's boys' group gets their safety badges at church. And the picnic here afterward."

"I remember." A smile came to Allie's face. "I'm so proud of him. He's come so far in a year."

"Yes." Ma raised an eyebrow. "We should all be doing so well."

Allie ignored the jab.

Ma stood. "I'm going to finish making salads for tomorrow."

Allie stood, too, and couldn't stop the groan that came to her lips. "I'll stay and help you instead of going to Shannon's for our Scrabble game."

Ma shook her head. "No, ma'am, you won't. That's your weekly ritual. You go take a hot shower. That'll help the stiffness. Then go on and play Scrabble." Ma reached out and squeezed her arm. "Honey, you never allowed yourself to grieve. You became stoic and just kept working. So did I. Too many losses in such a short time. For both of us. Now we need to move on with our lives."

Move on? To what? Still, Allie nodded her agreement. "Yes, I do know." She wanted nothing more than to protect her mother and Danny, but instead she was acting like a petulant child, mad at everyone around her and mad at God.

❧

Derrick grabbed the phone directory from a drawer in the hotel bed stand and leaned back against a stack of pillows he'd jammed behind his head. The luxurious room in the Marcus Whitman Hotel provided everything, including a wireless connection, but he preferred the yellow pages. He thumbed through the book until he reached the listing for churches. Since coming to the Lord, he rarely missed services, and then only due to circumstances beyond his control. Now he felt a special need to worship. More so because his good intentions were keeping him from being totally up front with anyone.

Oh Lord, I'm doing this for Sandy. She wants to know her son is safe.

The town's churches were limited, and he couldn't decide which to attend. He shut the phone book, got to his knees on the plush maroon and beige carpet, and bowed his head.

"Lord, I need Your guidance. Lead me in Your ways. Show me a church to attend. And I know You despise a lying tongue. I ask Your forgiveness for omission of truth. I want to keep Sandy's secret and remain a godly man. Only by Your grace and mercy. Amen."

Derrick stood. One niggling concern taunted him. What if someone recognized his last name and put him together with Sandy? Although that probably wasn't likely since eight years had passed between the adoption and now. His stomach growled a protest, and he glanced at the clock. Five thirty. Time for dinner. He headed downstairs to The Marc Restaurant, which the hotel attendant had promised was one of the best in town. Once he'd been seated and served, and after one bite of the succulent steak, Derrick reminded himself to thank the attendant for his recommendation. He adjusted the cloth napkin on his lap and tried to put his thoughts in order.

Okay, what had he learned so far? Derrick sliced his steak, then took a sip of tea. At this point it seemed likely that Danny Vahn was his nephew. Sandy had been living on the streets as a runaway, but when she realized she was pregnant, she'd gone to a clinic run by a religious organization. Different churches provided volunteers, and that was where Sandy had met her son's adoptive mother, a nurse named Cindy Vahn. She'd convinced Sandy that her best option was to give up the baby. A local law firm handled the private adoption, and the lawyer's name was Paige Maynard. Derrick sighed. A case could be made for coercion, based on what Sandy had told him, but. . .that was then. This was now.

So where did that leave him on his mission? How would he meet Danny's adoptive parents and be able to observe their interaction with the boy? All he wanted was to reassure Sandy— and himself—that Danny was in safe hands. If the boy's parents were anything like Allie, he and Sandy had nothing to fear.

Derrick finished up his meal, paid his check, and headed out of the hotel. He strode aimlessly around the center of town, his stomach in knots. He'd eaten too much too quickly. Perhaps a walk would settle his stomach.

Though Walla Walla was not very far from the dry arid desert of the Tri-Cities where his family lived, it was like a green oasis. He appreciated the sight of the Blue Mountains in the distance, where he often skied in the winter. Had Danny ever skied? It would be great to have an opportunity to teach the boy everything. To make him a part of the Owens firm when he grew up. . .

No. What was he thinking? He had to keep his promise to Sandy. Check on Danny, leave town, and report back to her. His nephew would never be a part of his life.

After passing one tourist-type shop after another, Derrick found himself several blocks from the hotel, wandering up Second Avenue. He was about to turn around when a junk store snagged his attention. Piles of items littered the sidewalk outside. Just the type of shop he used to visit with Lynn, the woman he thought he'd marry. The gaudy sign read THE QUAINT SHOP, and Derrick peered through the window at a washboard like his great granny used to own. He peered inside the store and caught sight of Shannon, Allie's friend.

five

Shannon had mentioned she owned a store. This must be it. For some reason it suited her. And having access to her alone suited Derrick. Maybe he could pry some information from her.

He wasn't two steps into the shop when Shannon came bounding up to him, a bright smile on her face.

"What do you know?" she quipped. "The hero's here!"

Derrick glanced over his shoulder. "Where?"

Shannon laughed. "It's time to close. Let me lock the door and you can join me in the back kitchen. I'm brewing tea. Want some?"

She twisted the key in the lock, then guided him to the back of the store before he could answer. Shannon pulled aside a beaded curtain, revealing a small kitchen with a tiny white table and two chairs. She pointed at one. "Sit. And don't worry, this is herbal."

Derrick eyed the delicate-looking antique chair and proceeded with caution.

"That is stronger than it looks, believe me." She held the kettle over a plain brown teapot and glanced at him. "None of that caffeine in this. Kills the liver, you know."

"That'll be fine." He'd be willing to put his liver on the line for a strong cup of coffee right about now, but it was more important to be sociable.

While she hummed and brewed tea, he studied the kitchen. Shannon had been born in the wrong decade. She would've been right at home in the golden era of hippies. He sniffed and scanned the room to locate the source of the strong scent.

"Jasmine and chamomile," she said as she poured tea from the pot to mugs.

He blinked. "What?"

"What you smell. Aromatherapy. Jasmine and chamomile. Good for end-of-the-day relaxation."

"Oh," he murmured. How had she known what he was thinking?

Shannon shoved a stack of papers aside and set a smiley face mug in front of him. "I'm thinking of expanding—opening a new shop in the Tri-Cities. Could be lucrative, I'm not sure."

"I might be able to help you." The words slipped out. He couldn't imagine a shop like hers in the upscale areas he serviced.

"Really?" Smiling, Shannon took a seat across from him.

"Yep. My father and I own a real estate company." He took a sip of tea. Weird.

"That would be totally awesome." She scooted to the edge of her seat. "Wow, what you did today. . ." Shannon sighed. "You saved my best friend from breaking something serious, that's for sure." She sipped from her cup.

"I'm sure Allie would've gotten that horse under control. She looks like a strong, capable woman." A memory of the wild-haired Allie atop the crazy horse made him smile. Allie was spunky, but something in her green eyes told him she was vulnerable, too.

Nodding, Shannon set down her cup. "Allie is capable, all right. And strong. I don't think I could've survived what she went through."

"Why? Are you afraid of horses?"

Shannon shook her head. "Oh, I didn't mean the horse incident. I mean she's emotionally strong. First her daddy died. He had a heart attack. No one saw it coming, although he was a lot older than Allie's mom." Shannon shook her head. "He was such a great guy. Anyway, then her brother and sister-in-law in that awful car accident."

Derrick held his breath—and his tongue—while he watched her slowly sip the tea. He couldn't hold back. "Danny's parents are dead?"

Tears pooled in Shannon's eyes. "Poor little guy. Allie made sure he got counseling." She jumped up, opened a cupboard door, and grabbed a box of tissues. As she peeled away the plastic from the box, Derrick scrubbed his jaw with his fingers. Danny seemed to be in good hands.

"Sorry." Shannon sat back down and blew her nose into the tissue, then fanned her flushed face with her hand, a silver ring on nearly every finger. "Anyway, Allie takes better care of everyone around her than she does herself. She might have done with some counseling as well." Shannon blinked, then looked at him as though she were surprised to see him sitting across from her. "Do you go to church, Derrick?"

What? The way her mind jumped from topic to topic could give someone mental whiplash. Patience. He had to get her to back up where she'd left off in the conversation, but again, his gut warned him not to push. "Yes."

"Oh, I had a feeling you were a Christian. I can usually tell. It's something on people's faces. . .well, really, it's in their eyes. The eyes are the windows to the soul, you know." Shannon's bright smile was back. "Derrick, you must come to Walla Walla Tabernacle tomorrow morning! Allie will be there, too. And guess what else. Tomorrow Danny's boys' group will get badges during the service."

Derrick quickly sorted through Shannon's words, keying in on the most important fact. He sent up a silent prayer of thanks. If it turned out Danny was his nephew, he'd be able to tell his sister that Danny was active in church. Sandy would be ecstatic. "In that case, I'm there. Where is it, and what time is the service?"

"Oh, cool! I've got last week's bulletin with the address." She got up and rifled through a three-inch stack of papers. "Here it is! Service starts at ten." Shannon gave him the bulletin, then rubbed her hands together. "It's like you're part of the family already, saving Allie's life and all."

Guilt speared his heart. He had to keep playing his part, keep up the facade, despite the fact that it meant leading on such nice people. "Got anymore tea?" He had forced down the strange brew, but he needed a reason to linger and keep Shannon talking.

Shannon was out of her chair, kettle in hand. She grabbed a tin can of. . . Derrick squinted at the label. What was he drinking anyway? "Pu-erh?" He didn't mean to say it aloud.

"That's right," Shannon said with pride as she made him another cup. "Comes all the way from Yunnan." When she was done, she dropped into the chair, mugs in hand. "Oh, don't worry, that's a province of China, not a different planet." She laughed. "You're funny."

"Me? Why's that?"

Shannon scooted closer to the table. "I study body language. And, well, the way you held your hand against your stomach when you said 'pu-erh,' I could tell you worried about what you were drinking."

Actually he was surprised his stomach felt settled since he'd drunk the tea, but best not to contradict her.

"And there's more to you than what's on the surface." She studied him with clear hazel eyes. "Sometimes the Lord shows me things about people, I think. Sort of a discernment thing."

Derrick held his breath. He certainly hoped not.

"I think you're a good guy, Derrick Owens."

He didn't feel as relieved as he should. He was a man with a secret, which didn't quite add up to being a good guy.

". . .but there's something." A frown creased Shannon's forehead.

Derrick forced himself to relax and meet her gaze. "Everybody has something, don't they?"

Shannon's gaze scoured his face, and the wary look in her eyes disappeared. Derrick released a pent-up breath. As he started to relax, a hard rap on the back door gave him a start.

Shannon jumped from her chair and went to the door. "That's Allie." She tossed him a sly grin. "She's come to play Scrabble."

And Shannon hadn't warned him? That meant Allie probably didn't know he was here either.

Allie stepped through the door, and her gaze slammed into his.

"Look who's here," Shannon said with a gleeful smile.

"I have eyes." Allie's smile wobbled. "I'm surprised to see you, Derrick."

"No more surprised than I am to see you," Derrick said dryly.

"One more for Scrabble. It'll be fun." Shannon looked like a kid in a toy store.

Allie drew a deep breath. "Sorry to be rude. It's good to see you again."

"I was wandering the streets after dinner, getting a feel for the town, and I saw Shannon in the store. Decided to come in and see what's up."

Shannon set a third cup of tea on the table. "Derrick is going to help me find a place to rent in the Tri-Cities for my expansion shop."

"Oh?" Allie raised an eyebrow in his direction.

"I'm a Realtor. Property is my business. I handle rentals as well as sales."

Shannon pointed. "Allie, sit. He doesn't bite." Shannon grabbed a worn Scrabble game from the top of the refrigerator.

Allie blushed and dragged another chair to the table. Derrick hid his smile with his teacup.

"Did your mother tell you the good news?" Shannon glanced at Allie as she dropped the box on the table, pulled out the game board, and unfolded it.

"She sure did," Allie snapped.

Shannon pressed her bejeweled hand to her throat. "Does it upset you that she'll be working here?"

"Upset me? My best friend is definitely moving and didn't let me know. And she hired my mother and didn't tell me? What do you think?"

"I'm sorry. I thought I told you." Shannon patted Allie's arm. "I was just so involved with all the decisions, I wasn't remembering everything."

Derrick could believe that.

"Well, you didn't." Allie tapped the table with more vigor. "Ma is already working, cleaning the church. I worry about her. I don't want her working so hard."

"Come on, Allie. It's not like she's senile or something. She's not *that* old. I think she can make her own decisions." Shannon handed out letter holders.

Irritation lit Allie's eyes. "I know that, but I'm allowed to be concerned about my own mother, aren't I? She's been through too much. I want to protect her *and* Danny. She's always worked so hard. I just want to take care—"

Her jaw snapped shut, and she glared in Derrick's direction. Obviously his presence had slipped her mind.

Shannon grabbed Allie's hand. "Please understand. I'm hoping she'll be able to work here full-time soon. Manage the place. That means she can stop the cleaning job. In the long run, that will be easier on her."

Allie inhaled, and her shoulders sagged. "Okay. I give up. You're right." She lifted one corner of her mouth—a poor effort at a smile.

Shannon took game pieces out of the box. "And it will be lucrative, too. I'm going to work it out that Betsy gets a percentage of sales. That'll help you guys pay—"

"Let's talk about it later." Allie slid another quick glance Derrick's way.

A distress signal shot through him that went beyond just caring for his nephew. It was concern for the petite farrier and her mother. He tried to stifle the feeling. He couldn't afford to get deeply involved. Yet their well-being did directly affect his nephew. And the things Allie had left unsaid raised some doubts in his mind. How could he pursue this without giving away his real purpose?

Derrick sighed inwardly as Shannon began to pass out Scrabble letters. He got the letter *X*. No matter. Perhaps he'd earn extra points by using the word *pretext*.

six

A high-pitched blare startled Allie from sleep. She jolted forward in bed, her heart pounding. "Wh–what?" Was someone playing a poor rendition of reveille? Early morning sun glowed around the edge of her blinds. She scanned the bedroom through slit eyes, focused, and caught sight of Danny's dress shoes poking out from beneath floor-length curtains.

"What in the world?" Allie glanced at the digital clock. It was eight thirty. She'd forgotten to set her alarm. "Daniel James Vahn!"

Allie pulled back the covers, got out of bed, and groaned from stiffness. She tiptoed toward the window where the muslin curtain billowed, then settled back, outlining her nephew's wiry form. "Danny? You little monster." She poked at where she thought his shoulder would be.

Danny giggled. His face appeared between the two curtain panels. "It's Sunday morning. You were oversleeping. I had to wake you up."

She smiled but might've cried. He was growing so quickly. At almost nine, his facial features were more defined, emphasizing his coal black eyes. Before long he would be a man. A striking man.

He stepped forward, shedding the curtains like a cloak. Dressed in his uniform, he held his dented bugle in his left arm like a soldier and saluted her.

Allie planted her hands on her hips. "Soldier, that horn is for camping with the boys' group, not for use at home."

"Yes, ma'am." He snickered.

She bit back a smile. "Now skedaddle so I can get ready."

"Ma'am, yes, ma'am." Danny saluted again and hurried from the room, closing the bedroom door.

43

Allie sank to the edge of the bed and put her face in her hands. She hadn't rested well, tossing and turning, between worry about finances and the memory of Derrick. Playing Scrabble with him had been fun, with his bright smile and quick wit. Definitely a charmer and clearly a confident man. Michael had been that way to a degree.

While engaged to him she'd thought how nice it would be to marry and give Danny a family again—a mom and dad. Her heart ached for the losses Danny had suffered. He deserved better than he'd had in his life. She often wondered about his biological mother, but knew nothing except the little her sister-in-law Cindy had told her. His mother had been young and living on the street. She couldn't give him what he needed.

That was ironic. Allie was beginning to think she wouldn't be able to provide for him either. She stood and stretched. With so much debt left by Luke, she was on the verge of declaring bankruptcy. She wanted to give Danny a secure life. In her heart of hearts, she knew her mother was right.

"I've been proud and stubborn, Lord." But she had her reasons. She'd do anything to hide the extent of their family problems from outsiders. She wanted to protect Luke and hide what he'd done. Lying, keeping a second set of books. . . her own brother. But why had he done it? What could have driven a man who was otherwise so honest in his dealings to lead a double life? Worse, she had to admit she felt betrayed by the Lord. Why had He allowed so many bad things to happen?

She clasped her hands and closed her eyes. "Lord, we need answers. If You're really there, if You really do watch over us, please give me answers."

Forty minutes later Allie forced down bites of toast in the kitchen while she tried not to think about Derrick. *Stop it!* she told herself. Why was she dwelling on a virtual stranger? The phone rang and put a stop to her ridiculous train of thought. She snatched it off its cradle and barked, "Hello!"

"Allie, it's me. I forgot to tell you last night that I invited. . . so I. . .and he. . .then I. . ."

"Shannon?" Allie pressed the phone closer to her ear. "I can barely hear you."

"Oh. . .won't hold the cell to my ear. . ." Shannon said something else that Allie didn't catch. "Just read. . .same as sticking your head. . .microwave. Brain cancer."

Allie huffed out a sigh. "Well why can't you wait until we get to church?"

"No! This is important!" Shannon's voice came through loud and clear. "Did you hear the part about Derrick coming to church?"

"What?" Heat burned her cheeks. Just when she'd been dreaming about him.

"I invited him last night, but I forgot to tell you."

Allie ignored the footsteps coming into the kitchen and focused on the phone conversation.

Shannon giggled. "I think he likes you, Allie. All that time we played Scrabble, he kept trying not to look at you. You know how I'm good at reading body language—"

"Shannon! Why did you invite him to church? I'm not interested in a man right now, no matter what his body language says. You remember what I went through nine months ago with—" She turned to see her mother standing in the doorway.

"Michael? Forget about him!" Shannon said. "You need to leave that in the past and move on." The timbre of her voice had changed to the one she used for animals and small children, making Allie feel stupid. "Besides, Derrick coming to church is really not that big a deal. If anything, we're being kind to someone who's temporarily in town. What harm can come from it?"

Ma cleared her throat, and Allie faced her, pointing at the phone.

"Shannon, I'm not—"

Ma pointed at Danny then at her watch.

"I have to go," Allie said.

"Okay. I'll talk to you at church." Shannon's voice was too cheerful.

As she hung up, Allie could have sworn she heard her friend laugh, and a bolt of irritation raced up her spine. She switched her attention to her mom. "Let me brush my teeth real fast."

"Okay. I take it the hero will be at church today?"

"I guess." Allie shrugged. "Thanks to Shannon."

"He will?" Danny smiled widely. "Yay!"

"Hurry, then. We'll be waiting for you in the car." Ma and Danny walked out of the kitchen into the utility room and then outside.

As Allie hurried to the bathroom, she mentally scolded her friend. Shannon had arranged this on purpose. Now there were three people set on matchmaking. Her mother, Danny, *and* Shannon, and she wanted no part of it.

&

As Allie walked down the church aisle, her eyes burned and she glanced up at the wooden ceiling beams to hide her tears. Hard as she tried to please the Lord, to love Him, she was at odds with Him lately. Her anger caused her lack of faith in His goodness, and she couldn't find a cure for it.

I'm sorry, Lord.

Trailing Ma and Danny, Allie shuffled into the pew four rows from the front and sat at the end next to Danny. Her gaze automatically roamed to the second row. Shannon. They locked gazes, and Shannon winked, then she smiled at Ma and Danny.

Allie turned at the tap on her shoulder. She found herself staring up into Derrick's dark eyes, unable to utter a solitary word.

Derrick smiled. "Good morning."

His crisp shirt dazzled white in contrast to his tanned skin and black hair. She grew as breathless as yesterday when he yanked her from Chester's back and into his arms.

"Mr. Derrick!" Danny grabbed Derrick's attention, saving

her the mortification of revealing her inability to form a coherent sentence, a rare occurrence.

Derrick greeted Danny with a warm smile. "How are you, Spiderman?"

"Great. This is my granny." Danny pulled on Ma's hand.

Allie's face heated. She should've made the introduction, but Derrick had her so tongue-tied, she'd forgotten her manners.

"Derrick," Ma said, "it's a pleasure to meet you. I'm Betsy Vahn. Please call me Betsy. Thank you so much for rescuing my daughter yesterday."

"I told Granny you're a hero," Danny added.

"And he told me all about hero school." Ma's grin was wide. "If we'd known you were coming, we would have saved you a seat." She leaned forward, indicating with her eyes that the pew was filled, and shrugged.

"Quite all right." Derrick pointed to the front. "Shannon saved me a seat."

A spot near Shannon? Allie felt a spurt of jealousy, then told herself to get over it. She wasn't interested in any man. Not now. Not for a long time. But despite her mental self-chastisement, she watched as he walked over to sit beside her best friend.

Allie's cell phone vibrated in her purse. She fished it out, peered at the text message on the screen, and saw Michael's name. ALLIE, WE NEED TO TALK. The man wasn't listening to her. She didn't want to talk. She wanted nothing to do with him.

The music commenced, and Allie stuffed the phone back into her purse and rose with the congregation, but her gaze kept returning to Derrick's broad shoulders. He seemed to know the songs by heart—not once looking at the lyrics on the overhead projector. She caught a glimpse of the side of his face. Eyes closed and hands lifted, he appeared to be sincerely worshipping God. Allie leaned forward, caught her mother looking at her, and swung her gaze to the screen. Great. Ma was grinning.

What was there to grin about? Who knew anything about Derrick Owens? Charming, friendly, and more than likely a professing Christian, but experience had proven even people she'd known a long time couldn't be trusted.

❧

As the pastor wound up his sermon and asked the boys' group to come forward for the special ceremony, deep sadness washed over Derrick. Sandy should be here. She should see this boy who was her blood. He had to find an opportunity to snap a picture of Danny to show his sister. Though Allie and her mother obviously loved the boy, he had to get close enough to check if he was being raised in a good environment. Just to ease Sandy's mind and, if he was truthful, his own.

He couldn't resist turning his head to observe Allie and her mother. Betsy was tall and blond with brown eyes, so different in looks than petite Allie with her auburn hair and green eyes.

Allie met his gaze, and Derrick turned toward the front and looked at Danny. So many details pointed toward Danny being his nephew, like his age, birth date, last name, and the mention of a Paige Maynard that Derrick had heard yesterday. But Danny's eyes cinched it for Derrick. Black like his own and Sandy's, a trait they'd inherited from their father.

Derrick tugged at his tie. A part of him wanted to talk to Paige—the woman who had taken advantage of Sandy when she was only nineteen. But as much as he resented the lawyer and wanted to give her a piece of his mind, he reminded himself he had to keep his promise. Talking to Paige might lead to Allie discovering who he was and his relationship to Danny.

The pastor asked for the parents of the boys to come up.

Derrick's heart felt like it was cracking. Danny's parents were gone. His biological mother was slipping away, too. He fisted his hands and forced himself not to stand and take part in the ceremony.

But Allie ran up to stand beside Danny. Her face shone with love. Derrick couldn't pull his gaze from her. Something he'd never felt before put his senses on high alert. This feeling. . .it wasn't familiar to him. He'd dated many women, beautiful women. But Allie. Perhaps he was looking at her heart, far past the physical, warm and inviting.

She caught him staring, but he made no attempt to hide that he was watching her. Their gazes entwined, just for a moment, and his heart thundered in his chest. He had to get out of town. Fast. Before anyone discovered the truth. And before he lost his heart to a woman he could never have.

Danny left his friends to hug Shannon, then high-fived Derrick before running from the church.

"That kid's like lightning," Derrick said, glancing over at Shannon. "Thanks for inviting me to the service."

"I'm so glad you were able to make it. Danny is something else." Shannon's eyes searched his face and lingered. "Isn't he?"

Had she seen a resemblance between himself and Danny? "Yes, he's a great kid."

"I've often wondered about his real family. They have to be awesome." Shannon half smiled and patted his arm. "I've got to run. Will we see you again?"

"I don't know," Derrick said. At least that was the total truth.

"Okay." Shannon turned abruptly and ran smack into Allie. "Hey, Al. You know what the Bible says, right? 'In all things God works for the good of those who love him, who have been called according to his purpose.'"

Allie fidgeted with her purse strap. "What are you talking about?"

Shannon glanced from Allie to Derrick. "Just keep it in mind."

Danny bounded back into the church whooping and made a beeline for them.

"Shh," Allie motioned with her index finger on her lips. "This is a church."

Smiling, Danny bounced on the balls of his feet. "When are we leaving?"

"Shortly." Allie combed her fingers through Danny's dark hair. "I was so proud of you today."

"Thanks, Aunt Allie, but I'm really hungry. Can we go—"

"Allie, I'll see you in a little while." Shannon pointed her thumb over her shoulder. "You should invite Derrick to the picnic today."

Allie opened her mouth to speak, but her mother spoke first.

"What a great idea, Shannon." Betsy's eyes were warm. "The boys' club is coming over for a barbecue and potluck. You come, too. It'll be my thank-you for rescuing Allie."

Allie's head snapped toward her mother, and her brows lifted.

"Cool! Please come." Danny nodded enthusiastically and tugged on Derrick's arm.

How could he refuse the boy? "All right, then. I'll see you there," he said, which earned him an unreadable glance from Allie.

seven

Derrick pulled his gray Silverado into the Vahns' driveway and sat behind the steering wheel, strumming his fingers on the dashboard. He shouldn't be here. He was getting too emotionally involved—and not just with Danny.

Even if an argument could be made for coercion when it came to Danny's adoption, that point was moot now. Sandy only wanted to know her son was safe and happy. She didn't want his life interrupted. Yet here Derrick sat in front of the Vahns' house, wanting to spend time not only with his nephew, but also with Danny's aunt, both of whom he'd be better off never seeing again. No way could he have a relationship with Allie. Wishing that things could be different only made the situation more difficult. He hardened his resolve to get a picture of Danny. That done, he'd walk out of his life—and Allie's—forever.

As Derrick strode up the gravel path to the house, he couldn't help but view the property with a real estate agent's eye. It was habit after years in the business. Despite the obvious efforts of the two women to keep things up, the property had a run-down air. The gardens were neat and tidy, but all the buildings needed a coat of paint, including the house. The land around the house was pretty. Flat fields with clumps of trees here and there. Some of the outbuildings in the back were falling down, but the barn remained in good shape.

He scanned the old, single-pane glass windows. From his periphery, he thought he saw Allie staring out one of the upstairs windows, but when he looked again, she'd gone.

No more stalling. Derrick rang the bell, and Danny was at the screen in two seconds flat. "Mr. Derrick!" He swung open the door with a warm, welcoming smile.

"Danny." Derrick gave the boy a quick hug and was rewarded with the feel of his nephew's arms around his neck, a bittersweet experience that he tucked away to cherish as a memory.

They stood in a tile foyer, and a long hallway spread out in front of them with a wide staircase on the right. To his left through an arched opening was a formal living room. Derrick surreptitiously studied the old farmhouse, which he judged to have been built in the early 1900s. Everything was neat and tidy and so clean. He would find no dust balls in the corners. But the furniture was dated and the sofa threadbare. Old water stains marred the ceilings. Signs of decay would be evident, even to someone without a practiced eye.

Derrick walked farther into the room, and his breath caught in his chest. There, on top of a spinet piano amidst an array of framed photos, was the same picture Sandy had given him of her son with his new parents. Only this one was larger and framed with gold.

"Come on," Danny said, tugging at Derrick's arm. "Let's go outside through the kitchen."

Derrick ripped his gaze from the picture to follow Danny. As they started up the hall, Betsy entered through a doorway at the other end where he could see a kitchen. She strode toward them, carrying a piece of paper.

"Derrick! I'm so glad you made it. Allie is upstairs. She'll be down in a minute." She held up the paper. "I've made a sign for the front telling everyone to go around back and join us. That way we don't have to keep answering the door."

"Yes, good. . .good idea." He had to get his bearings. He felt overwhelmed and couldn't think straight. If only Sandy were strong enough to be with him now.

Betsy taped the sign to the door, then turned to her grandson. "Danny, Pastor John is heating the grill. You go out and make sure he has everything he needs. I'll be out in a minute."

"You come, too, Mr. Derrick," Danny said as he bolted

down the wood-floored hall and disappeared into the kitchen.

"Be right there." Derrick kept in step with Betsy's slower pace.

"This house is old," Betsy said, her tone apologetic. "It needs more work than we've been able to do."

She must've noticed him checking things out. "Oh, was I gaping? If so, I'm sorry. I love old houses and tend to imagine renovations here and there."

"That's fine. I understand." She sighed as they walked. "My husband never had time to do much. He was too busy with the family blacksmith business. Nor did we have the money to do a lot of renovation. We still don't."

"A lot of people find themselves in situations like that." Derrick wanted to kick himself for whatever she'd read on his face that had her making excuses for the condition of the house. Perhaps his facial expressions were too like his father's. A man who tended to look down on those who weren't in his social stratum.

The front door banged open. Betsy whirled around, and Derrick glanced over his shoulder.

Michael, the man he'd met at the parade, walked into the foyer.

"Oh," Betsy whispered. "I'd forgotten Michael was coming. Let me introduce you."

"We've already met. At the parade." Derrick couldn't help the irritable tone of his voice. He hadn't liked Michael at first glance and didn't like him any better now. But he was worried the reason was jealousy, and Derrick hated that emotion.

Betsy must have noticed. She sent him a fast glance. "Oh. Well then, please excuse me. I need to say hello."

Derrick let her go and made a quick exit into the kitchen. Since Paige was Michael's sister, there was always the possibility he would mention Derrick to her. And despite the passing of almost nine years, she might recognize his name and tell Allie or her mother. He could only imagine the hurt in

Allie's eyes if she discovered he had misrepresented himself to her, Betsy, and Danny.

In the kitchen he skirted a large oak table covered with bowls and platters of food to reach the mudroom. There he exited the house onto a cement slab that served as a back porch. Under a large maple tree, Danny and the pastor were working on the grill, and Danny waved but was immediately distracted by one of his friends. People stood or sat in groups talking. No one paid much attention to him. This was a perfect time to snap a few pictures and just observe. He walked over to another maple, partially hiding himself, and held his phone up until he could see Danny on the display screen, then snapped. He took two more, glanced up, and noticed the spectacular view of the Blue Mountains in the distance so took a few shots of them, too.

"Taking pictures?"

Derrick jumped, almost dropping his phone. Shannon stood at his elbow.

"I love the scenery here," he said quickly.

"So it would seem." Shannon tilted her head.

"I don't have a view like this at home." Derrick opened the viewer on his phone and showed her the pictures he'd taken of the mountains. All the while his mind screamed, *Liar!*

❧

Allie stayed upstairs as long as she could. Lack of sleep caught up with her, and she wasn't in the mood to see anyone, yet she had to go face a houseful. She'd watched Derrick arrive and then Michael. Their joint presence alone was enough to make her feign sickness. But she couldn't do that to Danny or Ma. And she had to start the burgers.

She ran down the stairs to the kitchen and took a platter of raw burgers from the refrigerator. A shadow fell over her, and she turned and saw Michael.

"You're avoiding me." Michael crossed his arms like he expected an explanation. "I saw you hide behind your truck before the parade."

Allie felt sheepish, but nodded, tired of pretense. "That's an accurate statement. I am."

Michael's blond brows drew together. "Why's that?"

"We broke up." Allie placed the platter on the counter with a sigh. "You were dating another woman when we were engaged. That's called betrayal."

"That's called a *mistake* on my part." The muscle in his jaw worked. "And I'm sorry it happened."

"Admitting it was a mistake and being sorry don't mend betrayal. Not for me. You were living a lie."

"Something I'll regret the rest of my life."

The pain he felt was obvious, but his duplicity had almost destroyed her. Allie shook her head. "I found you kissing another woman. Then you told me you weren't sure what you wanted—"

"I wasn't sure, but that made me realize it's you I want. Only you, Allie."

"If you weren't sure, you shouldn't have gotten engaged to me to begin with. I'm sorry, Michael." Allie picked up the platter. "It's over."

He drew closer. Too close. "Who's this Derrick?"

"Exactly who he said he was. A businessman passing through town."

"Then what's he doing here at the picnic?"

"Not by my invitation, and none of anyone's business."

Anger flashed in Michael's eyes. "Are you going to tell me you don't love me anymore? That you can forget what we had between us?"

Had he always been petulant and pushy, and she just hadn't seen the real Michael?

"There is no 'us.' It's over." She walked toward the screen door, but he jumped in front of her and held it open.

Outside she headed for the grill manned by the pastor. Ma stood next to him chatting. Michael hovered near the back door and began to chat with a local family, much to her relief. Allie studiously avoided meeting his gaze.

Pastor began to put burgers on the grill. "I'm not an expert, but your mother asked me to do this."

Allie shrugged. "You'll be fine. Thank you for doing it." She was relieved. She wouldn't have to man the grill. The way she felt today, she'd probably burn the burgers to a crisp.

She glanced around, not wanting to admit to herself she was looking for Derrick. She finally spied him with Shannon, nose to nose in conversation, partially hidden by a tree. Her legs felt frozen, and she couldn't tear her gaze from the picture in front of her.

Shannon's long hair hung free, blowing in the breeze. Her light skin and hair looked striking next to Derrick's dark hair and tanned complexion. How humiliating to feel jealousy over a man who meant nothing to her! Her cheeks heated. A good thing God allowed people's thoughts to stay private— but what was in her heart? Pining over Derrick Owens, a total stranger?

Ma joined her. "Honey, you look like you've been sucking lemons. What's wrong?"

"What *isn't* wrong?" Allie snapped.

"Allie," Pastor John said. "How about we sit and talk?"

Allie dropped onto the bench and held back a sigh. Everybody knew that a "talk" with pastor meant a serious sermon. Why couldn't she keep her feelings to herself?

"Your mother was telling me about your financial situation."

Allie shot her mom a withering look. Great. On top of everything else, now everyone would know the Vahns were headed for bankruptcy.

The pastor smiled and touched her arm. "I know it's hard to share things like this, but we need each other. We can agree with you in prayer that God intervene and do a miracle."

"Seems we've been a little short of those lately," Allie blurted before she could stop herself.

Ma opened her mouth to speak, but Pastor continued. "I understand why you would say that. I don't have any pat answers for you. I wish I did. However, God is still in the miracle business. He still answers prayers."

And there in a nutshell was Allie's biggest issue. If God still answered prayers, why were things so difficult for her? For Ma and Danny?

But for her mother's sake, Allie agreed. They bowed their heads, and she tried to listen, but her thoughts were too loud. She wanted to believe. She wanted to return to the strength of faith she'd had several years ago, but her relationship with the Lord had been eroded by her experiences. Michael's faithlessness. Luke's deception. Luke's and Cindy's deaths. Logically she understood the Lord wasn't a puppet master. People made their own choices. Things happened based on those choices. But she still felt let down, and she'd grown cold in her faith. So why would God respond to her prayers now?

eight

After the picnic Allie was cleaning the kitchen with Shannon. Through the window over the sink, she saw Derrick and Danny helping Ma roll the grill to the old shed in the backyard. Odd. . .he looked so familiar, like he belonged.

"Michael didn't stay long," Shannon said.

"That's because I told him under no uncertain terms that our relationship was over. Completely over."

Shannon snorted. "You've done that already."

"And already and already and already," Allie said. "He seems to think dating another woman behind my back was just fine as long as it led him back to me."

"He's justifying himself." Shannon loaded the last glass in the dishwasher. "Like if his bad actions led to a good result, it's okay."

"Yeah." Leave it to Shannon to analyze the situation. "And it's not just that he did it or tried to justify it. The thing that bothers me most is he's never admitted it was wrong. He said it was a mistake and he was sorry, but sorry for what? That he got caught? It's almost as if I should be glad it happened because he ultimately decided I'm the right girl for him."

"I'm not surprised." Shannon wagged her head. "I never liked him, as you know. He was too good for a lot of the simple things in life. He would never have stooped low enough to drink my tea or play Scrabble with us."

Shannon's words were true, and she was sure her friend meant to point out a fundamental difference between Michael and Derrick. Michael was a snob. Derrick wasn't. Funny that would be so obvious even though they hardly knew Derrick at all. Or maybe Shannon was getting to know him better than Allie thought.

"I'm a fine one to talk about being snobbish, though." Allie shoved a plastic pitcher of juice into the refrigerator.

"What do you mean?" Shannon scowled. "You're nothing like Michael."

"Maybe not, but I have my own issues." She glanced at her friend, then at the floor. "I'm pretty mad at God right now, along with people—men—I can't trust."

"Oh, that. Don't worry." Shannon waved her hand in the air. "The key is to keep the communication open with God. Don't stop talking to Him. Ask for forgiveness. He'll deal with your heart, and the feelings will follow."

"I suppose." Shannon's encouragement didn't assuage her guilt; it only made her irritable that her best friend had an easy friendship with God. And maybe the picture in her head of Shannon and Derrick didn't help. "What were you and Derrick talking about earlier?" Allie inspected the countertop like the question meant nothing to her.

"Business," Shannon said, not looking up.

Allie attacked the sink with cleanser and a sponge. "What kind of business?"

"Yours and mine." Shannon dried a pot and put it in the cupboard. "I told you he's going to help me find a property to rent in the Tri-Cities, right?"

"Yes." That meant Shannon and Derrick would be working together. Allie felt the stab of jealousy again and shook her head. Ridiculous.

Shannon gave her a sidelong glance. "We also discussed your situation. He might be able to help you sell some land."

"That again?" Allie slapped the sponge into its plastic holder behind the sink. "Why is everyone talking to everyone else about my personal business?"

"Gee, that's an overstatement. I only meant to—"

Ma, Danny, and Derrick walked into the kitchen, all three laughing. Then Ma held up a rectangle of paper. "The pastor gave us a check, Allie. It's from a fund at church for parishioners in situations like ours. It will help get us through this month."

Allie wanted to shush her mother in front of Derrick. Not everyone needed to know their financial woes.

"Derrick!" Shannon flapped a dish towel in his direction. "Tell Allie what you said about the land."

Derrick dropped onto a kitchen chair, looking as if he'd been a part of the family forever. "I might be able to help you sell part of your land. I have a buyer looking for investment property—possibly to subdivide and build houses. That's why I'm in town."

"And that's not all." Shannon motioned for him to continue.

He nodded. "I thought you could give me a quick tour of the place. I'll go back to the office and poke around a little bit, look at other listings, run some figures on comparable properties. Talk to some people. Then if things look good, I'll have to come back for a longer look."

Allie swallowed. When all was said and done, she didn't want to sell. Especially to someone who was going to build a subdivision. She loved her home and the privacy it afforded them. But what choice did she have?

"Go show him around before it gets too late." Ma stuck a card on the refrigerator with a magnet. "Derrick's business card."

"I'm coming outside with you!" Danny crowed. "I want to show Mr. Derrick the barn."

Ma and Shannon exchanged quick smiles, then stared at Allie expectantly. No need to wonder why Ma hadn't shown him around the property herself. She was matchmaking again, which was more than useless. Derrick was here on business, which was becoming more apparent by the second. There was the possibility that he'd already looked into properties and saw theirs as a good prospect. The thought occurred to Allie that maybe he was using them for his own ends.

Danny waited near the door, and her heart ached for him. He'd been attached to Michael. Looking back she realized

Michael had given Danny attention until Michael had won her heart, then he'd backed off. Danny had noticed and kept trying to win Michael's approval to no avail. She could never allow that to happen again. Danny was vulnerable, and according to his counselor, going through a stage where he was searching for a father figure. Even now he waited impatiently, eager to show Derrick around. How could she protect her nephew? In just a day and a half, Danny had developed a bond. She couldn't bear to see him hurt again.

Derrick glanced at his watch. "I'll probably need to leave soon. I have to. . .um, I have another appointment."

Another appointment? Is that what he considered his visit with them? An appointment?

Allie tried to smile. If she were honest, she'd developed a bit of an attachment to Derrick, too. She chided herself for weakness and pointed toward the door. "Let's get to it, then."

As they walked out of the house and toward the barn, the wind mussed his thick black hair, sending wisps across his forehead. Their fingers brushed, and she had the sudden thought that it would be nice to hold his hand. Fortunately, Danny jumped between them and interrupted her insane desire.

"Hey, Spiderman," she said. "Lead the way."

Danny bounded ahead of them. Their footsteps were silent as they crossed the yard, and the crickets sang their familiar song. Would she lose all this?

Derrick looked over at her. "So how did you get into the blacksmith business?"

"My dad started it. Learned it from his father. He taught me and Luke." Her breath caught. "He was my brother—"

"Luke was my dad," Danny said over his shoulder. "He's dead. So is my mom. And they're in heaven. There's no time there, you know. So while I grow up, they're happy and waiting to see me again."

Oh the simplicity of a child's faith. And of course Danny was listening to every word she and Derrick exchanged. They reached the end of the backyard and began walking the fence line toward the barn.

Derrick motioned at a cottage beyond the barn. "What do you do with that?"

"Nothing at the moment. We rented it out for a while, but it needs a lot of work, and we haven't had time or money to do it."

Why was she opening up to this virtual stranger? Perhaps Pastor's prayer had helped after all, but was Derrick a safe person to open up to? She waved to the right. "We lease out these fields to a local farmer. That brings in some money, but it's not enough. Not with the amount of debt we have to pay."

Derrick stopped and looked at her intently. "There's got to be a way to fix this."

If not for his serious demeanor, she would've been amused. "I assure you, my mom and I have tried everything."

He seemed to be waiting for further explanation, and Allie hastened to change the topic. She pointed at a small building next to the barn. "That's our. . .my office. That's where I take care of the business." She motioned for him to follow her to the weathered barn. When she opened the door, Danny ran ahead of them and disappeared through a doorway in the back—his hiding place. "Danny's favorite place is the barn. I hope we can keep it when we sell property."

"Oh man, this is tough." Derrick almost spoke the words to himself.

"Yes, well. . ." She inhaled the familiar scent of hay and straw, and tears stung her eyes. Two horses in stalls next to each other stretched their necks over the bottom half of the stall doors, and she rubbed the mottled gray face of the first.

"The horses love you, huh?" Derrick smiled.

"I love them, too." Allie moved to the second stall where a stocky bay horse snuffled gently against her arm.

"Do you have just these two?" Derrick reached out, stroked the horse, and his fingers trailed over her hand. She didn't move. The rough feel of his fingers warmed her skin.

"Yes. We had to sell the others." A lump rose in her throat. The time was coming when she might have to sell these as well and her heart would break.

"They're both quarter horses. The gray is Storm. This guy is Pip. I named him after Dickens's character in *Great Expectations.* My dad used to read that story to me. He bought me Pip when I was fifteen." She hugged the horse's neck and buried her face in his mane. "Pip has been like a friend to me," she said almost to herself. "I used to hang on his neck and cry during the worst of my teenage angst."

Derrick went to Storm's stall and patted his neck. "Beautiful animals."

Beautiful, she thought. Derrick Owens definitely cut a striking figure. "Do you ride?"

"Yes. Not as well as you, of course." His laughter sent a shiver of delight up her spine. "I can't forget your wild ride at the parade."

And she couldn't forget the feel of being in his strong arms. She found herself smiling despite the prospect of losing the land she so loved.

Derrick sobered and looked her in the eye. "Shannon said your father died of a heart attack."

"Yes." Allie stared out the barn door in the direction of the mountains. "Seems he had a ticking time bomb in his chest. We didn't know until it was too late. He was quite a bit older than my mother, but they adored each other."

"And your brother and his wife died in a car accident?"

"Yes. A terrible tragedy. Sometimes I relive it over and over again in my dreams. It had already been a bad day. They'd been fighting and. . .shouldn't have been on the road." Allie took a deep breath. "Well, anyway, thank God Danny wasn't with them. Last minute, they asked me to watch him."

"Yes, indeed," Derrick murmured and cleared his throat. "We should talk business. I know the thought of selling part of your property is hard. You appear to love it, and it's part of your family history. I understand that."

"Yes." Allie met his dark gaze to see if he was sincere. Those eyes—expressive and sensitive.

Allie switched her gaze to Pip, gave him one last scratch, then walked back to the door. She wrapped her arms around herself and stared at the Blue Mountains. Lately she'd felt older than twenty-eight. She worked long hours, and when she did take a break, she felt guilty. The responsibilities were always there like clanging alarms waiting to be turned off.

"What are you thinking?"

She hadn't heard him walk up behind her. He was so close she could turn and fall into his arms. Being held, having someone to lean on, would feel so good. She shivered. Would Derrick stick around long enough for her trust in him to grow?

"I'm thinking that Shannon has a point when she says we all need balance in our lives." Allie shrugged. "For instance, I love the mountains in the winter. I ski. Cross-country. I pack food and just go all day. Sometimes Shannon goes with me, but she chatters too much." Allie snickered. "Though I couldn't ask for a better friend, sometimes I need the solitude. But when I do it, I feel selfish taking time for myself."

"I don't get the chance to feel guilty. My dad's the travel agent for guilt trips."

Allie laughed. "Is he?"

"Oh yeah." Derrick's eyes crinkled with a good-natured smile. "But I understand your need to be alone." His voice was low, like he was confiding secrets. "When I want to be alone, I hike into the bare hills around the Tri-Cities. I sit and stare out over the Columbia River. I also ski."

"Shannon and I are going on a spiritual retreat next week. At a monastery. We have to spend part of our time in silence."

Derrick chuckled. "That will be hard for Shannon."

"Yes it will," Allie agreed, then she shuffled her feet on the floor. "I write poetry."

"Poetry?" Derrick's raised brows told her he was surprised. "Really?"

The heat of a blush inched up her face. "It's silly really, but writing poetry helps get my feelings out."

"Not silly at all." Derrick clamped his hands behind his back and looked her in the eye.

"Mr. Derrick!" Danny yelled from the back of the barn. "Come and see my hiding place."

Allie's heart pounded hard, and she was relieved by Danny's interruption. "You go on. I'll feed the horses. He'll enjoy showing you his treasures. Danny is so much like Luke, even though he was adopted. From a little boy, Luke would stash things in hiding places. Anyway, when you're done, tell Danny to bring you to my office."

Derrick headed toward the back of the barn, and despite her efforts to resist, she drank in his retreating form. He looked capable and strong, like he would protect the people he loved. For a dangerous moment, she found herself longing that Derrick Owens would fall in love with her.

nine

Sunday evening Derrick hovered in the doorway to Sandy's bedroom, trying to muster the courage to face his sister. This was his "appointment" that he'd mentioned to Allie and her family. He needed to tell Sandy everything he'd discovered.

The decor was so like her. Creamy yellow walls, bright white curtains open wide to let in the light. The room glowed, even in the dark of night.

He clutched the bouquet of flowers in his hand and stepped through the door. His mother rose from a blue cushioned chair next to Sandy's bed and came toward him. It seemed Mom had aged overnight, and he hoped his face didn't give away his concern. Dark roots were visible through her usually perfect blond hair. Lines carved around her eyes and mouth had appeared during the last month.

"Mom." He gave her a peck on the cheek.

"So glad you're here," she said. "Sandy ordered me to wake her when you arrived."

His sister looked pale and thin under her covers. "Please don't. I can come back later."

"I think we should do what she asked."

Because we don't have much longer to do it, Derrick completed his mother's thought while he fought tears. His mother wouldn't cry. His parents never did, at least not publicly. They regarded stoicism as admirable, to be worked at and sought after like some people worked at getting fit. His father alleged that displays of emotion made one vulnerable. Something others could use as tools to manipulate.

Derrick sighed. He agreed in part, but there was a time and place for emotional expression. To allow loved ones to know how much they were cared for. He'd seen and felt it this past weekend in Allie, Betsy, Danny, and even goofy Shannon. Allie was the one who withheld the most, but even she showed depth of emotion with her poetry, her horses, and her love for her family.

"Mom is right," Sandy's weak voice came from the bed. "You'd better do what I ask."

"You're not asleep; you're just pretending." Derrick crossed the room, smiling. "And what are you going to do if I don't do what you ask?"

"Don't mess with me, D-man. You know I have ways of getting even."

The light banter helped relieve the knot of dread in his stomach. No matter how ill, Sandy's sense of humor remained.

She pointed to the flowers. "Wow. A girl has to be dying for her brother to pay attention to her."

"Sandy!" Mom hissed. "What a horrible thing to say."

Sandy laughed softly. "Why should I deny it, Mom? I *am* dying. Laughing makes it easier to cope."

"I find nothing funny about it." Their mother edged toward the door. "I'll leave the two of you alone. Your father will be here soon; I'm going to wait for him."

Derrick watched his mother slip from the room, her high heels tapping hard on the wood floor of the hallway as if clicking their disapproval.

He placed the flowers on the nightstand and sat on the edge of the double bed. "Did you do that on purpose? To get rid of her?"

Sandy shrugged. "Not really, but I'm relieved. I feel bad for Mom. She's really struggling with this, but she acts like I'm already dead, walking around on tippy toes, turning off my happy worship music when she thinks I'm asleep, and putting on this heavy, funeral dirge classical music. As if she's afraid anything lively is going to kill me more quickly."

He laughed and cried at the same time.

Sandy's smile lit her eyes, making it easier to look at her thin, pale face. "The hospice nurse has been coming in. . .

Leanne. She's wonderful, and we conspire together and think up practical jokes."

That was so like her, the joker. He feared if he took a breath, the tears he fought would come in a flood.

Sandy took his hand. "It's okay. You can cry. In fact, do anything you need to do. God's biggest gift to me is the realization that He isn't just a stern God, but He's also a loving Father who wants His children to enjoy life. We're allowed to laugh and even get mad. Sometimes I'm so mad at God, I could just spit." She sighed. "Yeah, I know. Some church people would tell me that's horrible. I should never be mad at God, but He knows my thoughts, so I might as well admit them. Mostly I'm peaceful. I'm beyond grateful I had the opportunity to be born again. And even better, that you and I were born again at the same time."

The memory of the altar call they'd answered together was clear, like a series of snapshots in his mind. Sandy's street-hardened expression had melted into peace, taking years off her face.

Derrick swallowed past the hard lump in his throat and kissed her forehead. "It's so good to see you." He pulled the worn picture of Danny as a baby with Cindy and Luke from his shirt pocket. "I wanted to return this."

"Thank you." Sandy pointed to her Bible on the bed stand. "Put it in there and tell me everything. All about this young man who is my son."

"I have good news, and I have bad news."

"Of course. That's always the way, isn't it?" She poked his arm. "So get on with it. I really don't have forever."

"Okay, here's the good news. His name is Danny. I'm positive he's your son. I saw a larger version of that picture you gave me on top of a piano in the living room of their house." Derrick tucked Sandy's copy in her Bible.

"Danny." She smiled. "Short for Daniel."

"The bad news. His parents are dead."

Her eyes widened. "What? How?"

"Car accident. A little over a year ago. Now he lives with his aunt and grandmother." Derrick pulled his phone from his pocket. "I have some pictures. I took these at a picnic at their house today." He went on to explain about Danny's award at church while she flipped through the photos. "And I have a surprise for you."

"You do?"

He pulled a photo from his pocket. "This is Danny and his grandmother. I e-mailed it to myself and printed it out for you."

"Wow, look at my handsome son. Aw, his grandma looks sweet." Sandy glanced up. "Whoa, D-man, I just realized what you said. You got invited to a picnic at their house? How?"

He grinned and saw himself pulling Allie from the horse. "I guess you could say it sort of fell into place." He explained in detail about the parade, meeting Shannon, playing Scrabble, and being invited to church. Then he explained about Michael and expressed his worry that Paige might recognize the Owens name.

"Maybe. But how many people have the last name Owens? She'd need good reason to tie you to Danny. Do you have a picture of Allie?"

Just the mention of her name sent a rush of adrenaline through his veins. "No, I don't." Derrick squinted at the photo for all the diversion was worth.

"I see. And she's not married?"

"No." Derrick massaged his forehead, hiding his eyes from his sister. Their relationship had always been close because they were together so much as children, tended by a nanny while their parents worked long hours. That bond gave them rare and precious insight into each other's thoughts.

"Danny," Sandy said softly. "Like Daniel, the Old Testament prophet. A man with great faith and conviction."

Derrick nodded. "His eyes are dark like ours."

"Danny's family are good people then."

"Real good people. Danny's Aunt Allie and his granny love

him. . .adore him. But they're struggling financially." Derrick looked directly into her eyes. "A big part of me wants to do something. Intervene. He's family. He's our blood. I want him to know, and I want to help take care of him."

Sandy shook her head violently. "Derrick, no. The family has been through so much. A boy losing his parents and then just when he finds out he's got a biological mother, she dies, too? That would be cruel. And then there's Dad. If he found out, there would be no peace for Danny's family."

Derrick said nothing. Knowing Danny as short a time as he had, he wasn't sure the boy would struggle, at least not for long. But Sandy was right about their father. "I feel dishonest. And now I have to go back."

Her mouth fell open. "You're going back?"

"Yes." Derrick clarified about the Vahns' land. "Danny phoned me on my way here. He invited me to his birthday party next Saturday night. I've woven a tangled web." Derrick couldn't help but think of Sir Walter Scott's words, *"Oh what a tangled web we weave when first we practice to deceive."*

Sandy was quiet for a moment, then drew a ragged breath. "It's risky, you know, but the land is a good way to help them. And I know you want to see Danny again. I want to see more pictures if you can get them. Close-ups."

"The Vahns could discover I'm a fraud, I suppose." A big part of him wished it would happen and save him the pain of an explanation. The more time went by, the harder it was to keep up the subterfuge.

Derrick squeezed Sandy's frail hand. "Are you sure you don't want them to know? I mean, the way you gave up Danny. . .I'm not sure it was on the up-and-up. At the very least, it was coercion. They took advantage of a young, drug-addicted woman."

"We've talked about this. No." Sandy's voice was surprisingly strong. " 'In all things God works for the good,' you know."

Strange, Shannon had said the exact same thing.

"The thing is, D-man, I couldn't have cared for Danny at

the time. I was living on the streets. And I was on the outs with Mom and Dad and was afraid to face them with my story. Now, looking back. . .well, he wouldn't have been raised in a Christian home. Mom and Dad weren't. . .aren't. . ."

"I know." He and Sandy prayed for their parents. They thought their childrens' conversion to Christianity was an annoying but passing phase. "Remember when Dad said we were in a cult?"

Sandy laughed and shook her head. "Oh, it's not funny really." She pointed at him. "Have Pastor Clark officiate at my funeral. If anybody can bring down the conviction of the Holy Spirit. . ." Sandy's face lost all animation. "Seriously, if Mom and Dad hear him preach, they've got a real chance of coming to the knowledge of the saving grace of Jesus."

"If Jesus takes you home, I'll do that."

" 'If,' huh?" Sandy blew out a long sigh. "There's no 'if' about it."

Derrick wanted to argue, but he couldn't. Instead he vented his anger at the disease that was killing her. "Why cancer? You could have fought the hepatitis."

"I talked to the doctor about that. Hepatitis makes a person more vulnerable to lymphoma. Talk about reaping what you sow. I was in such a drug haze back then. I didn't care about anything but my next fix."

She grabbed his hand. "I was a fool. I didn't even know who Danny's father was. Could've been anyone, probably a dealer. I was a charity case in drug rehab. Scared to death. But God watched out for Danny. Cindy came along. She was a volunteer nurse at the clinic. She wanted a baby badly. Said she and her husband had been trying for a long time. She said if I agreed, she would adopt my little boy, and she seemed like an angel at the time. I never saw Cindy again, and before Paige disappeared, she gave me that picture I lent you."

"I'd still like to tell them the truth, sis."

Sandy raised his hand to her cheek. "Remember Danny's namesake? God protected Daniel even in the lions' den. His grace is sufficient. I'm dying, Derrick. Please let Danny be. God will take care of him." A little twinkle lit her eyes.

"Now what?" Derrick frowned. "You're up to something."

"Tell me about this Allie. I think you find her attractive."

Derrick leaned back on the bed and huffed out a sigh. Just as he'd dreaded, Sandy had seen through his facade. "It doesn't matter. She can't know who I am, remember?"

Sandy's smiled died. "Yes, that's true."

"I'm invited back next weekend for Danny's birthday party, and I'm going to inspect their property and see what I can do for them. Then I'm going to disappear from their lives."

"I'm sorry." Tears came to Sandy's eyes. "I can tell you like this woman. Maybe more than like her?"

Derrick shrugged. "There are lots of women." His statement was ironic. He'd always said that after ending relationships in the past because no one had ever captured his heart. But this time the words felt hollow. Allie wasn't like the others. For the first time in his life, he realized he was truly capable of falling in love—deeply, madly, and forever.

ten

On Tuesday afternoon after she'd shoed the Armstrongs' two palominos in preparation for a show, Allie sat in her truck and consulted her planner. As she scanned her to-do list, she nodded. "Looking good." She and Ma had worked out their schedules with Mary, the mother of one of Danny's friends, so he could be cared for while Ma trained at Shannon's shop.

Shannon. What would she do without her best friend? Tears pricked the backs of her eyes, and her nose burned. Another loss. It seemed the Lord saw fit to strip her of everybody and everything she'd given her heart to.

Allie drew a breath and shook her head. She was just feeling sorry for herself. She still had Ma and Danny. They were more than enough to be thankful for. They were her life. Her reason to get out of bed in the morning and keep going.

She swiped a tear from the corner of her eye, returned her attention to the planner, and groaned. She had to check on Eddieboy, Frank Johnson's cranky pony, who was recovering from a bad case of thrush caused by a poorly cleaned stall. Frank, who was almost as cranky as his pony, could have treated the thrush himself, but Eddieboy was not cooperative, to say the least—one of the reasons he was often left to his own devices in his polluted stall. He had an enormous set of teeth and wasn't hesitant to use them.

Allie tossed the planner on the passenger seat and started down Highway 12. If she survived her encounter with Eddieboy, she'd call on Raymond Connor. He ran a stable of trail horses and had given the Vahns business for years. But after Luke died, Raymond had moved on to another farrier. He didn't believe women should be farriers, let alone work *outside* the home. Losing the man's business had been a hard financial blow. If only she could convince him that a woman was just as capable as a man.

"Good luck with that." Allie flicked the turn signal and hung a right.

So much to do today. She would stop at the bakery between her other appointments to ask if they were on top of Danny's cake.

And last. . .she didn't have to look at the planner to see what she wanted to avoid at all costs. She'd prefer to deal with Eddieboy and his teeth than to hear that deep voice and try to act casual.

Return Derrick's call.

What luck that she'd been in the middle of an appointment when he'd phoned. Last thing she needed was to be caught off guard with nothing clever to say.

Allie grabbed her cell phone from her purse. She'd already heard Derrick's message, but she wanted to hear it again. "Hi, Allie, this is Derrick. I've got a quick question for you. Call me back."

She sucked in a breath. His deep voice. . .the way he spoke her name. . . An involuntary chill raced up her spine.

"Call me back," Allie repeated. As though any single woman in her right mind wouldn't return Derrick Owens's calls. The man was not only self-confident and good-looking, but also nice. Which is precisely what drew her to him and scared her all at once. She shouldn't waste her time. He was most likely only after her land. And she couldn't really fault him for that. He was a businessman. But he had the courage to save her at the parade. That said a lot for the kind of person he was.

Allie glanced at the clock on the dashboard. She wasn't due at the Johnsons' for an hour. Plenty of time to call the tall, dark hero.

She pulled her truck over to the side of the road, threw the gearshift into PARK, and rubbed her thumb over the clouded glass on her cell. Derrick was probably calling her with an offer. She'd either accept or reject. Nothing more to it. Then he'd walk out of her life.

"Oh, for Pete's sake." She had to grow up. Allie snapped on her headset, drew a breath, then dialed Derrick's number.

After three rings, her shoulders relaxed. He wasn't going to answer. She could leave a message and—

"Hello." Derrick's voice sounded close and intimate and sent a shiver of pleasure down her spine.

"Umm, Derrick. This is Allie. Allie Vahn."

"Allie." Was she imagining the smile in his voice? "I'm glad you called me back. I have a question for you."

"Sure. Fine." She readied herself for the worst. "Is this about selling my property?"

"No." Derrick laughed. "I want to get Danny a birthday present, and I wondered what he'd like."

A birthday present? Of all the things Derrick could've asked, this hadn't been on her radar.

"You don't have to do that." What was he really getting at? "Between myself and Mom and Danny's friends, he'll have plenty of—"

"I know I don't have to, but I want to. I'm not going to show up without a gift for him."

"Show up?" Allie pressed her hand to her heart. "Show up where?"

After a long silence, she shook the phone. Had their connection been severed? "Derrick, you there?"

"Yeah, um, this is awkward." Another pause. "On my way home on Sunday, I got a call from Danny. He invited me to his party. I assumed you knew."

"He called you?" Where had Danny gotten Derrick's phone number? Aha! The business card on the fridge. Smart boy. Wait till she got her hands on the kid.

"I'm sorry," Derrick said, "this should've been cleared with you first. I won't come."

"What? No, it's fine." Her heart hammered as hard as the day she'd nearly been thrown from Chester. "Danny invited you. But I want you there, too." Allie clamped her hand over her big mouth. What had possessed her? Heat traveled from her neck, into her cheeks, stinging the tips of her ears.

"Are you sure?" The softness of his voice seemed to suggest a deeper question. But she could be hearing what she wanted to hear.

She summoned her most casual tone. "Of course Danny wants you there or he wouldn't have called."

"As long as you're okay with it, I—"

"Of course. It feels like you're a friend of the family already."

"Thanks for that. So. . .any gift ideas? I'm not up on the latest for nine-year-olds."

"Hmm, I'm getting him a handheld game system. How about you get him a game to go with that?"

"Easy enough," Derrick said, and the background noises suggested she should make a graceful exit.

Allie cleared her throat. "I guess—"

"I've got to—"

They spoke at the same time.

"Sorry." Derrick laughed. "You first."

"I was just going to say I have an appointment, and I guess I'd better go."

"Sure thing. I'm about to head out to a meeting with a client who might be interested in your property."

"Oh, that's great," Allie lied.

They exchanged good-byes, and Allie snapped her phone closed. "What's wrong with me?" She rested her head against the steering wheel. Derrick ended the call with business, taking all the wind out of her sails. *Not that you're in the market for a man,* she reminded herself.

Allie shifted the truck into Drive and headed toward her next appointment, her stomach aching and a dull throb in her head. Even if she couldn't save herself from her foolish emotions, she had Danny's feelings to consider. The poor kid had attached himself to any father figure she'd brought home. Derrick Owens had been in town to find land for a developer.

She had Danny and Ma to consider. Time would tell if Derrick became anything else.

"Lord, if Derrick's got a fatal flaw, please reveal it to me. If he's nothing more than a real estate agent selling our land, please intervene and don't let us all get attached to him." Her prayer was heartfelt. Ever since Pastor prayed for her at the picnic, she'd found herself more expectant about God's answers. Slow but sure, she was beginning to give her life back to the Lord. To trust Him.

Trust. She didn't trust men, either, and she was surprised Derrick had wormed his way into her life so easily. Were she and Derrick two ships passing in the night? Allie sighed. She'd have to get it out on paper. She would have to write a poem.

&

Good phone conversation or bad? Derrick frowned. Today Allie had shifted emotional gears fast enough to make his head spin.

Laura ran up to him and grabbed his arm. "Mr. Owens, your dad wants you in his office. . .ASAP." His secretary's whispered command startled him from his deep thoughts.

Derrick nodded, then rounded the corner and strode down the long foyer to the end of the hall. Now what? Surely he'd be called to task for not giving a full account of his whereabouts. His mind raced, and he dismissed one lie after the other.

Well, Dad, I was at a picnic with the woman of my dreams. Spending time with my nephew.

Yeah, Derrick. That would definitely work.

He tapped lightly on the cherrywood door before entering. He turned the brass knob and approached his father's ornately carved desk on cat's feet. "You wanted to see me?"

His father continued to study the computer screen. "I've been waiting to hear about your trip to Walla Walla." He turned finally and looked up. "Land? Ring a bell?"

"I found a likely prospect." Allie's property. Danny's

home. Derrick took a seat in front of his father's desk. "It's farmland—"

"Good, good." Dad steepled his fingers, and his eyes narrowed. "Are we looking at a steal or a deal?"

He had once admired the real estate tycoon. Now the idiom made his skin crawl. Derrick shrugged.

"Don't disappoint me, son." He pushed back from the desk and stood. "I want to see *something* in writing." His face turned as crimson as Walla Walla's illustrious mayor's.

Derrick caught himself lifting his hands in a gesture of surrender, a motion he'd used so often through the years to placate his father. He purposefully lowered his arms. No more. "Nothing is settled. I've got to go back, do a bit more research before I—"

"For crying out loud!" His father paced like a caged lion. "First your sister, now you." He rapped his hand on the desktop. "Are you both going to turn out to be losers?"

Dad's words were harsher than normal and cut deeply. "I'm doing my job. I don't want to lose business by being careless." Derrick sprang from his chair. "I don't care what you think of me, but Sandy is no loser. She's a great kid. A little mixed up, but—"

"She's no kid." Dad sliced the air with his meaty hand. "And sure enough, neither are you." Breathing heavily, he clamped his hands behind his back. "What were you doing in Walla Walla all that time? Womanizing again?"

Derrick stood head-to-head with him, his face heating. Dad's attack today was worse than normal. He sent a silent prayer to the Lord for help. "I don't do that stuff anymore, Dad. And you know it."

"Sure, sure, you got religion." He wagged his head. "A zebra doesn't change his stripes."

Derrick's phone buzzed, indicating a text message. He glanced at the screen and put the phone back on his belt. "I have to go. That's my secretary. I'm needed." He turned and walked toward the door. Understanding hit. His father was stifling his grief about Sandy dying and taking it out on Derrick. He turned. "I'll keep you appraised of the Walla Walla details."

"I expect results that benefit us. None of this Christian namby-pamby stuff." Dad sat again at his desk. "And we'll speak again shortly."

The "results" would mean taking advantage of the Vahns. He'd taken advantage of desperate sellers before, raising his percentage by a few points with the promise of getting it done quickly. Could he do it again?

eleven

What a day. Allie headed up the highway toward home, the worst part of her day divided equally between playing keep-away with Eddieboy's teeth and her visit with Raymond, who'd told her in no uncertain terms that he was done with the Vahns' farrier service.

"A woman, 'specially one your size, couldn't possibly be a farrier. Your brother, now we're talkin' a horse of a different color."

But when Allie pulled into her driveway and saw Michael's BMW parked in front of the house, Eddieboy's teeth and Raymond's scolding looked inviting. She didn't want a showdown with Michael, especially at her house. But if she disappeared, Ma and Danny would be worried and hunt her down.

On a deep sigh, she parked her truck next to her office and went to the barn to clean her tools, taking her slow, sweet time about it. Would Michael ever give up? Her pulse quickened with anger as she loaded her tools back into her truck.

By the time she was walking toward the house, she was ready to take someone down. She stomped through the yard to the back entrance, stopped at the sound of Michael's voice, and inhaled deeply to gather her emotions, reminding herself that anger profits little. She stepped into the kitchen, and there Michael sat at the table, working on a 3-D puzzle with Danny and Ma, eating ice cream. Michael made a snide remark, and Danny laughed.

Allie dropped her keys on the counter, and once again fury rose from deep inside her. Michael was using Danny again to get to her. She approached the table short of breath.

Michael looked up and smiled. "Hey, Al. I came by to bring Danny a birthday present." He motioned at the puzzle.

"I invited Mr. Michael to my birthday party." Danny smiled.

Anger constricted Allie's chest, and she could hardly breathe. Before she said something she'd regret, she needed to escape and gather her thoughts. "I'll be back," she managed. "I have to change my clothes and shower."

She crossed the linoleum, heels of her boots thudding hard, feeling everyone's eyes on her back, and ran up the stairs to her room. She sent up a silent prayer for peace and took care not to slam her door.

❧

That evening Derrick paced the parlor, reliving his conversation with Allie.

"Will you be joining your parents for dinner?" Hank, the chef and all-around housekeeper, as well as one of Derrick's confidants, stood at a discreet distance.

Who could eat? "Hey, Hank. No thanks. Maybe later."

"If you need to talk, you let me know."

Derrick nodded. "Will do." He needed to be alone with his thoughts. Hank disappeared before he could offer an apology for his rudeness, and he added another regret to his growing list, but he couldn't bear to speak with anyone right now.

"Oh Lord, give me wisdom." Derrick went past the back staircase, bypassing the dining room unseen, and quietly walked down the hall. *Lord, help me sort this out.*

He dropped into a comfortable leather chair in the library and closed his eyes. He hated having to make choices, but this is where he'd found himself—in the belly of the whale. He could disappoint his father, although that was nothing new, or he could shortchange Allie and her family. Or. . .

He could confess all to his parents in the hopes that they'd understand. But that would mean betraying his sister. Going back on his word. Then there was Allie.

Derrick massaged his aching forehead. He lived in a different reality than Allie. He had no money worries, didn't believe money in and of itself was evil, and was grateful for the blessing now that he'd come to know God.

"Derrick?" His father strode into the library. "I thought I heard you. I'd like to talk to you before dinner."

He acknowledged his dad with a nod.

His father sat across from him on the sofa. "Have you seen Sandy?"

"Earlier today, just briefly." He held tight to his reserve. No emotions allowed.

Dad shifted in his chair. "Have you seen Lynn lately?"

Strange question and out of left field. "Lynn?" Derrick shook his head. "I haven't seen her in months."

A frown formed a V in the middle of Dad's forehead. "You stopped dating her?"

Sad. But if he'd taken the time to talk regularly, his dad would've known. "Yes, we broke it off. A mutual decision."

"Ah. I see. She couldn't take the other women in your life, no doubt."

Derrick focused harder on his father. He barely knew the man. He'd grown up watching him come and go and bark into the phone incessantly, happy when his dad tossed him a few crumbs of attention, wishing for so much more. But Sandy—Dad's negligence was hardest on her. He often wondered if Sandy's daredevil antics were to get attention from the man she called "Daddy dear."

"I want to discuss keeping the business in the family."

"It *is* in the family." Derrick tugged at his tie. Where was this leading? "It's you and me."

"Yes, and therein lies the problem." Dad stood and paced the room. "Your mother mentioned that the Victors recently had a grandson."

Understanding hit like a sledgehammer. "Are you suggesting I get married and have children just to carry on the Owens name?"

"You're thirty-two going on twelve." Dad scowled. "Aimless. Don't you feel it's your duty to—"

"Duty?" Derrick slapped his hand on the arm of the chair and stood. "I'm not going to be the king of England. Do you think I'd marry a woman I don't love so I can give you heirs to the business?" Even as he said the words, his thoughts went straight to Danny. This confirmed Derrick's feelings. He'd never be able to tell his father he already had a grandson. Worse, that meant he couldn't be honest with Allie. Sandy was right. Dad would never leave the Vahns in peace, especially now that Danny's adoptive parents were dead. Where did that leave the Vahns legally?

Dad crossed the room and stood directly in front of him. Odd that they could be so physically similar and yet completely opposite in character. Strangers, in a way. "Sometimes we need to do things that aren't comfortable because it's best for the family."

Where had Dad been when he and Sandy were young and needed him desperately? "I'm not listening to this. It's archaic at the very least, and it's demeaning." In the past his parents had hinted at their hopes that he'd marry and have children, but he couldn't remember a conversation that had been this blunt.

Dad blinked, and his eyes reddened. He ran his hand over the back of his head. "Family is everything, you know."

It might be too late, Dad. Derrick took a deep breath. "I understand that family is important." He'd seen that connection between Allie and her mom and Danny, and at least he'd experienced it with Sandy in the last few years after she'd returned home.

"Try to understand." Dad strolled to the arched window and stared out into the night. "Sandy. . ." He squared his shoulders and cleared his throat. "Whatever. We forgive and forget. But she can't give your mother and me. . ."

Derrick saw his father through new eyes. The hotshot real estate mogul had turned into a fragile, vulnerable man in a blinding flash.

"Dad." Derrick strode toward him and rested his hand on

his shoulder. Why hadn't he noticed his father disappearing before his eyes? Dad's independence and big personality had clouded his vision.

"Well then." Dad backed up. Derrick dropped his arm. "I'm glad we had this talk, son."

No. There was so much more to say—but Derrick stood speechless and watched his father leave the room.

❧

Allie awoke to the sound of knocking on her bedroom door. The room was dark, her hair damp and partially wrapped in a towel, and she was on top of her covers wearing a bathrobe.

"What?" She blinked and focused on her clock. Eleven-twenty. And this was. . .Tuesday night.

"Allie, it's Mom. I'd like to talk to you."

Allie switched on the lamp on the nightstand, tossed the towel on the floor, and sat on the edge of the bed. "Okay. Come in."

Ma entered and lingered in the doorway. "Were you asleep?"

"Yes. I guess I laid down for just a second and dropped off. I'm sorry." Sour memories came rushing back. "Is Michael still here?"

Ma shook her head and settled on the edge of the bed. "No, he left."

"Good." The word slipped out of her mouth before she could think straight.

"We need to talk." Ma smiled. "Are you up to it?"

"What about?" Allie combed her hair with her fingers. She would have to wash it again just to work out the tangles.

"Tell me what you're thinking."

Allie blinked. "Thinking? About what?"

"Your actions tonight were. . .rude."

Allie sat back, and the anger she felt when she'd seen Michael's car returned with a vengeance. "*I'm* rude? How can you say that? I walk into my own house after a hard day's work and find Michael sitting at the kitchen table as if everything is peachy. And you and Danny laughing and doing a puzzle with him. Gee, what's wrong with that picture?"

Ma's eyes flashed. "This is not just *your* house. Two other people live here who have feelings, too."

Allie's fury grew. "Michael was *my* fiancé. He cheated on *me*."

"Michael didn't come just to see you. He came by to give Danny a birthday present."

Allie shook her head like she'd been sucker punched. "Ma, that's pathetic." Her mother was sometimes naive when it came to people's motives. "I know you choose to see the best in people, but even you have to realize Michael's using Danny as a portal back to me."

"Then blame me." Ma shrugged. "I'm the one who invited him to stay awhile. I felt sorry for—"

"I thought you understood what Michael put me through." It was one thing for Ma to feel sorry for every repentant soul and quite another to invite Michael back into their lives.

"I do, but I felt bad for him."

"Are you implying that I should go back with him?"

"That's not what I said. Not at all."

Allie pulled in two long breaths. This was going to turn into a talk on forgiveness, and she had forgiven Michael, but she didn't want him to be a part of their lives. Next subject. "Why did you let Danny invite Michael to his party?"

"I didn't. Danny blurted that out. I couldn't very well say no, even though I didn't think it was appropriate given the circumstances."

"Did you know that Danny also invited Derrick to his party?"

"Did he?" Ma smiled. "I had no idea. How did you find out?"

"Derrick told me."

She chose to ignore her mom's blatant show of pleasure at the prospect of having the hero attend Danny's party. "I know we've spoiled Danny a bit. He's the center of our lives, but we can't let him run things around here, either."

"Danny meant well." Ma sighed and stood. "He's a sweet,

sensitive kid. I sometimes look into his dark eyes and think. . ." She crossed her arms over her midsection. "Ever wonder what his biological parents were like?" She moved toward the door. "We could ask, I suppose, but Cindy said the records were closed."

I wonder all the time, Allie mused, but she'd save that conversation for another day. "All right, we'll make the best of it, but don't blame me if things go haywire with Michael at the party."

"You're bigger than that, sweetheart." Ma opened the bedroom door then turned. "So Danny really invited Derrick to his party?"

Allie grabbed a pillow and held it high over her head. "Another word about Derrick and—"

Before Allie could hurl the pillow, Ma ducked out of the room, laughing.

What did Danny have in mind, inviting both Michael and Derrick? Allie tossed aside the pillow and headed to the bathroom, her mother's query hanging at the back of her mind. *"Ever wonder what his biological parents were like?"*

Lately, and for no known reason, the question wouldn't leave her alone.

she crossed her arms over h...   ...tion. "Ever wonder what
he his real parents were...   ...moved toward the door.
The child had ...   .and the results were

twelve

Sunshine streamed into the kitchen window. Allie poured batter into the pan to make another batch of pancakes. Saturday. Danny's birthday.

"Allie!" Her ma's voice gave her a start.

Spatula in hand, Allie swung around. "I'm making pancakes."

"You didn't have to tell me. I followed the scent from my bedroom." Ma laughed and sidled up beside her at the stove. "Drown mine in syrup."

"Drowned in syrup, coming right up."

Her mother peered at her with a suspicious smile. "You seem very happy today."

"I am." Allie carried the two plates to the table. "Where's Danny?"

She needn't have asked. He thundered down the stairs and through the hall, skidded into the kitchen, and posed dramatically with his fists planted on his sides, hero-style.

"Do I look any different?" Danny puffed out his chest.

Allie exchanged a wink with her mom, then frowned and looked him up and down. "I don't think so."

Ma shook her head. "Except maybe your entrances are getting noisier."

"My muscles are bigger." Danny flexed his skinny arms, and she and Ma laughed.

"You're the light of our lives, kid." Allie set two plates stacked with pancakes on the table. "Now sit. Time to eat breakfast."

Danny bounced his fists and planted them harder on his hips. "Don't you remember what today is?"

"Today? Ma? Isn't today Saturday?"

"I believe it is. And I'm very hungry."

"Come on!" Danny yelped.

Allie laughed and pointed at his place at the table. "Silly boy. How could we forget? You've been reminding us for weeks now. That's why I made your favorite breakfast."

His ear-to-ear grin warmed her heart.

"Cool. I'm starving." He yanked back a chair and hopped into it.

Allie brought her plate to the table, and after they prayed, Danny began a litany of all the people coming to his party. She almost choked when her nephew mentioned Derrick's name, and she felt Ma's eyes on her.

"He's coming, right, Aunt Allie?"

"Yes. He said he'd be here." She sipped her juice, lids lowered. Her mom would surely be able to read her internal reaction. Allie focused on slicing her pancake. She was looking forward to hosting Danny's party. Her pulse kicked up a notch. And too eager to see Derrick Owens. In her head she wondered if his only motive for showing interest in her was part of his sales pitch. In her heart she wondered if there was more.

She'd better get her eyes off Derrick and a grip on reality.

"I almost forgot," Ma said. "Derrick called me this week needing information about the property." Her voice was light and cheery, as though losing the land Dad labored so hard to keep up was a simple necessity. There had to be other options. "He's going to be here this morning to pick up paperwork from me. Then he said he'll return for the party at five."

Allie's appetite fled. "Why didn't you tell me?"

"I didn't think it mattered much." Ma shrugged. "He won't be here long. So what are your plans this morning? Do you have appointments?"

"No, I'll be getting ready for the party. I've got to get caught up on paperwork, too. And I've decided to begin my long-term project of going through the old files in the file cabinet to clean them out." *In preparation for selling the property*, but she didn't say that. The pancakes tasted like sawdust.

A knock at the back door gave her a start. Allie's heart pattered erratically as Danny ran to get it.

"Mr. Derrick!"

"Hey, Spiderman. Happy birthday."

They came to the table smiling, and Allie was suddenly struck by the similarity of their eyes. Both coal black. The one difference was that dark circles hung like half moons under Derrick's. In fact, tension lined his face, making him look a bit weathered, which didn't take away from his good looks. It made him appear less polished and more human.

"Aunt Allie made pancakes." Danny pulled out a chair. "You wanna eat with us? Please?"

Ma greeted Derrick with a bright smile.

Derrick glanced at Allie as if gauging her reaction. She stood and pointed to the table. "We have plenty. I'll get some for you."

"Thank you." He slipped into the chair. "I already grabbed a bite, but pancakes are my favorite."

"They're my favorite, too." Derrick exchanged a high five with Danny then, head tilted, appraised Allie. Had he caught her staring? His gaze gave away nothing.

"If it's not too much trouble, Allie, could I have a cup of coffee?" His yawn said how badly he needed caffeine.

"Oh, sure." She piled a plate with buttermilk pancakes, her senses reeling, and set it in front of him and got the coffee. Her stomach felt like it was wrapped in a rubber band.

Danny, Ma, and Derrick held a lively conversation, but his presence turned her mind to mush, and she had trouble following their words.

"Delicious. Thank you." Derrick laid his fork on his plate, took a gulp of coffee, then cleared his throat. "Now, let's talk business. I need to look at the property more closely, take some notes. Nobody has to accompany me, but I need about an hour."

Ma stood. "Danny and I are off to pick up his cake and party supplies. Allie has paperwork to catch up on. But please, have another look around. If you need anything, Allie will be in her office."

"That works."

Allie felt heat in the sidelong glance he sent her way. She quickly averted her gaze, met her mother's eyes, and saw the faint smile on her lips. Matchmaking again.

❧

Derrick explored the cottage with land developer Les Links in mind. Les probably wouldn't be interested in the old cottage on the Vahn property unless it could serve as a decorative landmark. Too bad. It would be a shame to knock it down.

When he'd completed his inspection, Derrick dusted off his hands and pulled a notebook from his pocket. Now he'd have a report to show his dad. He sat on a tree stump beside the door and scribbled out notes, listing the pluses and minuses of the acreage. He worded his report in favor of restoring the cottage possibly as a community meetinghouse.

He eyed the building. The Vahns hadn't been able to keep it up. Weeds and plants grew in abundance. In the backyard was a massive blackberry bush that held berries just getting ready to ripen. Fixed up, the place would also make a nice home, smallish but charming, especially for a couple just starting out. But a developer wouldn't do that.

A couple. His conversation with his father slammed into his mind. Most of his adult life he had fought a serious romantic relationship. The closest he'd come was with Lynn. His parents welcomed Lynn with open arms. His mom wanted a grandchild and his dad an heir to Owens Realty. But when he'd made a decision to live for Christ, Lynn rebuffed his beliefs.

No matter. Derrick sighed. What he had with Lynn wouldn't have carried them through "till death do us part," especially with the fundamental difference in their faith. And worse—or better—he realized he hadn't loved her with a depth that would last a lifetime.

Now Allie...

Derrick got to his feet and stuffed the notebook into his pocket. Allie was unlike any woman he'd ever met, and they shared the same faith. He couldn't deny the growing attraction between them. But what about Michael? He still couldn't figure out Allie's relationship with the guy.

He glanced back at the building next to the barn that served as her office. He wanted to see her again, spend time alone with her. He had to find an excuse.

Derrick rubbed his hand over his jaw, searching his mind. Hmm. He could ask her permission to drive his truck into the field to look at the far end of the property.

A plausible request, he told himself as he strode up to her office door and knocked. He heard no sound coming from inside and rapped his fist against the door, a bit harder this time. He was about to call her name when he saw movement from the side of his eye.

Allie appeared around the corner of the building holding a bridle in her hands. "Are you looking for me?" Her voice was shaky and her face pale.

"Yes, but I didn't mean to disturb you. Um..." He suddenly felt awkward, like he'd intruded on a very private moment. "I'd like your permission to take my truck into the field to check out the pond."

She studied him for a moment, frowned, then seemed to reach some kind of conclusion. "I was about to go for a quick ride. Want to come along with me? You can ride Storm. I'll show you the boundaries myself."

What brought this on? Derrick agreed, too quickly perhaps, but he was more than pleased by her offer. Perhaps he'd misread the panic on her face a minute ago. Still, the cheer in her voice sounded forced.

As they saddled and bridled the horses in relative silence, Derrick stole glances at the petite, auburn-haired beauty. At least the color had returned to her face, but something in her eyes clued him in that she was troubled. He could easily imagine her mixed feelings. She loved the land she lived on. Sellers weren't always happy to see real estate people at their door—not when the sale was necessary to their financial survival.

"You ready?" Allie mounted. She looked regal atop the bay quarter horse.

Smiling, Derrick climbed atop Storm, and they took off at a leisurely pace into the field. A flock of birds flew up from a group of trees in the distance, and Pip danced a few steps.

"Derrick," Allie called over her shoulder.

"What?" He lagged a distance behind her. She was by far a better rider than he.

"I'm going to run."

Without waiting for his response, she lightly kicked Pip's sides. As if the horse had been hoping for his cue, he shot forward like he was leaving a starting gate. Storm didn't need much urging to follow, and Derrick felt the exhilaration of the wind in his face. Allie's hair blew behind her, and he loved the sound of her laughter floating on the wind.

For the first time since he could remember, he felt at peace, thinking of nothing but the moment. Allie radiated an inner beauty that had unlocked something deep and hidden in his heart. A tenderness he hadn't known existed.

As they neared the pond, Allie slowed Pip to a trot, then a walk. Following her lead, Derrick brought his horse alongside her.

"Beat you." Allie smiled.

Derrick pretended to scowl. "Are you kidding? I let you win."

Laughing, she stopped under a knot of trees and swung from Pip's back in one fluid motion. Derrick dismounted, too, and she took Storm's reins from his hands and tethered the horses loosely to a tree.

"They won't go anywhere. Danny and I come down here for picnics and to fish." She grinned. "Even if we never really catch anything. Come on. I have something to show you."

She held out her hand, and he hesitated half a beat before he took it. The close physical contact sent a rush of warmth through him.

"I don't know how much longer we'll own this place, so I want to enjoy it while I can, and I love to share the beauty with friends."

Her voice trailed away. She glanced at him, then back at the pond. A warning cloud engulfed him. A true "friend" would tell the truth and nothing but. He'd come to investigate whether or not Danny was taken care of properly. He had to be dreaming if he hoped for romance with Allie. She'd toss him out on his ear when she discovered the truth.

Derrick squeezed her hand and resisted the urge to pull her into his arms, hold her close, tell her why he'd come to Walla Walla to begin with. But he couldn't—not without betraying his dying sister's last wish. The only way he could help her was to get top dollar for her property. He glanced at her profile. Her pert nose and full lips. High cheekbones. What he wouldn't give to hold her, kiss her. . .

"Here we are." Allie led him along a path overgrown with plant life where the air grew cooler under the trees. They reached the pond's edge, and Allie turned to face him.

"So many memories." Her voice was resigned. "Daddy used to bring Luke and me here. Taught us both to fish. Then Luke and I did the same with Danny."

The catch in her voice tore at his heart. Derrick looked into her eyes. A stray tear zigzagged down her cheek.

"I feel like I've failed them," Allie whispered and backhanded the tear off her face.

He had to hold her, just this once. Derrick took her by the shoulders gently and looked into her eyes. "Please don't cry. We'll pray together that things work out and God will make a way for you and your family."

If only he could confess everything. Right now. *I'm Danny's uncle and—*

"Would you please hug me, Derrick?" Her jaw worked and then she swallowed. "I haven't had a big-guy hug in a long time."

She was asking for a hug? "Of course." Derrick pulled her against him, wrapped his arms around her slim shoulders, and inhaled the lilac scent of her hair. Is this what falling in love felt like?

She leaned back and looked up. She was so close he could see the kaleidoscope of shades that made up her green eyes.

"Thank you." She cast her gaze downward. "I don't really know you, but for some reason, I keep thinking I can trust you."

Derrick's heart pounded at Allie's words. She'd let down her walls, but he didn't deserve her trust. He slid his hand behind her neck. She glanced up at him, and her sweet breath feathered the corner of his mouth. He blocked the voice in his head urging him to tell her the truth. Leaning closer, he shut his eyes, touched his lips to hers.

Allie slipped her arms around his neck, and he held tighter to this woman who'd turned his world upside down.

He owed her the truth. But what about Danny? Sandy? Derrick pulled back, brushed his hands over her hair. "Allie," he whispered. "I. . ."

She nodded and closed her eyes, obviously thinking he was asking permission to kiss her again.

He proceeded to do so, and his runaway fervor shook him to his core.

Allie stepped back, and the expression on her face mirrored his infatuation. Surprise and wonder and. . .alarm.

She looked away first. "We should go back. I have work to do."

"Right." Derrick's hands slid from her shoulders, down her arms. He released her and instantly regretted severing their physical contact. "Good idea."

The ride home was quiet except for an occasional bird song and the twigs snapping beneath the horses' hooves. He had almost told her the truth. Only the kiss had prevented a confession from spilling from his lips.

They reached the barn, and Allie stared straight ahead. Her walls were back up. As were his own. He couldn't allow the intimacy to ever happen again. He had to honor what his sister asked, and his respect for Allie had to override what stirred in his heart.

Allie dismounted without a glance his way. He helped her remove the tack, then they quietly brushed the horses, avoiding being near each other.

"I'm sorry," he finally said, unable to bear the silence.

She shook her head. "It's not your fault. It's no one's fault." She glanced at him. "I'm not upset, I'm confused. I don't know what to think." She stepped backward. "I'll see you tonight at the party."

As she walked away, Derrick's heart felt like it had collapsed on itself and become a black hole. What had he been thinking kissing her? The relationship could go nowhere.

Lord, what am I doing here? Why can't I just walk away?

thirteen

Allie clutched a bundle of check stubs in her fisted hand and paced her bedroom. Why had she chosen the day of Danny's party to clean out the file drawer in her office? How she wished she'd never come across Luke's check stubs, hidden at the back of the bottom drawer behind their old financial records. Luke had handled the finances; she'd never had reason to go there. . . .

How was she going to tell her mother?

Allie went to her bed, lifted the mattress, and stuffed the evidence deep in the crevice. Her own brother. . . And to finally know why they were flat broke now. He'd been paying money to Paige Maynard. The amounts weren't huge, but over a period of years they added up to a hefty sum. Why had he been paying her?

The most likely scenario. . .

Allie closed her eyes and pressed her hand to her thudding heart. Could it have anything to do with Danny? His adoption? No. Danny's adoption was paid for years ago. What about an affair? Nothing else made sense. Back in high school, Luke had a thing for Paige, and Cindy, even in jest, had shown jealousy. Luke would scoff at the idea of it. Was that an act?

The thought of Luke cheating on Cindy—and with Paige Maynard of all women—made her stomach churn.

Allie went to the vanity, looked into the old glass mirror, and ran her index finger over her lips. Her intense state of shock must've driven her into Derrick's arms today. The old glass mirror darkened her reflection, and she closed her eyes and relived Derrick's kiss. Romantic. Tender. Like a whisper, yet tingly. The setting had been perfect. When she was a teenager with the whole world ahead of her, naive about the future, she'd often ridden to the pond with a book of poetry to read and a notebook of poems she'd written. She'd imagine the man she would marry, living on the farm, maybe in the cottage.

That young girl still lived inside her, and she struggled against the cynical woman she had become. *But I have to protect myself. . .don't I?*

She heard gentle tapping at the door. "Allie?"

She spun away from the mirror. "Shannon. Come in."

Her wacky friend opened the door, and Allie smiled at Shannon's outfit—a gaudy peasant dress in reds and earth tones accessorized by her ever-present silver rings, bracelets, and chunky necklace.

"Vintage?" Allie asked, pointing at her outfit.

"Yeah." Shannon turned, and the gauzy material swirled around her ankles. "I found a bunch of stuff at an estate sale a couple days ago."

"Very nice." The simplest pleasures made Shannon happy. Allie had often wished she was more like her friend. Content with the smallest things instead of so intense—so "on" all the time.

"I thought so, too." Shannon flicked back her hair and dropped onto Allie's bed. "Are you looking forward to our retreat this coming week?"

Allie nodded, although going away for several days seemed so unwise right now.

"What else is going on?"

Too much to tell. "Why does something have to be going on?"

" 'How do I love thee? Let me count the ways. I love thee to the depth and breadth and height my soul can reach, when feeling out of sight for the ends of Being and ideal Grace.' Elizabeth Barrett Browning." Shannon laughed. "A book of love poems *and* your Bible open on your bed stand. One of your poetry journals next to them. You're wearing your most favorite dress in the whole world, and you're makeup looks like it did when we drove to Portland and had that lady at the cosmetics counter do us up."

Allie blinked. "Wow. You're right."

"Has he kissed you yet?"

No, she'd kissed him first. "You are way too nosy." Allie paced the room.

"I'll take that as a yes." Shannon lounged on her elbow. "As much as I like Derrick, I think you need to slow down."

"What?" Allie barked out a laugh. "You telling the tortoise she needs to move slower?"

"Yes," Shannon conceded. "I guess you're right. You are slow." She sat straight on the edge of the bed and studied her face. "You both have walls up. I know where your walls come from and why they're there, but his. . ."

"What are you telling me?" Allie's face heated. "You're not going to start up with the body language stuff, are you?"

"All I'm saying is that it wouldn't hurt to find out a bit more about Derrick." Shannon got to her feet. "Come on, gorgeous. People will be arriving soon."

◈

Allie answered the front door, and her breath caught. She stared up at Derrick, speechless.

He stood there in a light denim shirt and dark blue jeans holding Danny's wrapped present and looking wary. "Am I too early?"

She touched her lips. Could she forget his kiss ever happened and at least make a pretense of nonchalance?

"I'm sorry. Come in, of course." She had trouble meeting his eyes, turned her back to him, and proceeded down the hall.

Derrick caught her by the arm. "I'm early because I want to talk to you alone."

Alone? Could she trust herself? She turned and finally met his dark gaze.

"Can you come outside? For a minute?"

She hesitated, then nodded. Derrick stepped back and allowed her to go ahead of him. The scent of his cologne made her long for his nearness. One more hug. . .another kiss. . .

"Listen, Allie."

They stood on the front porch, and she couldn't look him in the eye again. Instead she stared at the Blue Mountains.

Derrick touched her arm. "I'm sorry about what happened today. I want you to know it won't happen again. I promise."

Ouch! As much as she appreciated his honesty, it stung.

Derrick cleared his throat. "I'm no more ready for a relationship than you are."

"Direct and to the point. I admire that." Her hard shell thawed a bit, and with that came a smile. "It wasn't just you, Derrick. I was a willing participant, if not the one who initiated—"

"Hmm." His lips lifted in a half smile. "Let's just say we were both willing participants and leave it at that." He drew a deep breath. "Can we be friends? Pretend this afternoon didn't happen?"

She laughed, part of her wishing he'd declare his everlasting love, the other part knowing what he said was for the best—especially with Shannon's warning ringing in her head. "Yes. I agree. And this is Danny's birthday party. I want to enjoy myself."

"Good. I do, too." Derrick directed his hundred-watt smile her way, which threatened to be her undoing. Her insides turned to melting butter, and her knees weakened.

"I have another idea," Allie said. "Why don't I take you to Bright's tomorrow? I owe you some candy."

After the words left her mouth, she wanted to kick herself. Spending more time with Derrick was dangerous on her emotions. Her heart leaped while she waited for his response.

"Tomorrow?"

Allie caught sight of Michael pulling up in his BMW, and new worries knotted her insides.

Derrick turned to follow her gaze, then looked back at her. "Are you two—"

"No. No way." Her emotions must be so obvious. Now that Derrick had handed her the friend card, she may as well come out with the humiliating admission. "Michael and I were engaged. He cheated on me, then decided he wanted me back."

"He was a fool," Derrick blurted, and the words seemed to come from his heart. "Do you want to go back with him?"

Michael got out of the car, slammed the door, and walked toward them, a scowl on his face.

"No." Allie shook her head. "I can't abide lying."

A flicker of tension crossed Derrick's face. "Um, I'll leave you here. It appears Michael's not in the best frame of mind, and having another man with you isn't going to help matters."

Derrick disappeared into the house, shutting the door firmly before she could ask him to stay. Michael walked up the porch steps.

"Are you dating him?" He blew out a breath and strummed his fingers on his thighs.

"You can't say hello before you give me the third degree?" She was suddenly shaking. "I've had a long day. I don't need—"

"How can we talk? Whenever I see you lately, Owens is by your side."

The door opened again.

"Allie?" Shannon's voice came from behind her. "We need instructions to finish getting ready."

"Oh sure." Allie gestured for Michael to go inside. "I'm done talking. I don't owe you any explanations," she whispered to him. "This is Danny's birthday party, and he's the focus. If you must have a discussion with me, we'll do it later."

Michael opened his mouth as if to argue, then clamped it shut. He stepped into the house, and she followed. Waves of bitterness emanated from him, and she sent up a silent prayer that Danny wouldn't sense the hostility.

"Okay, more guests will be arriving soon," Allie said with

false cheer. "Let's get ready to party."

Shannon gave her a thumbs-up. Allie smiled, looked across the room, and met Derrick's gaze head-on. All tension drained from her, replaced by the foolish thought that everything would be all right as long as Derrick was around.

Derrick returned her smile, and she was totally entranced by everything about him. He studied her frankly, and his gaze dropped from her eyes to her lips.

At that moment she knew. She and Derrick could never be "just friends."

≈

After Danny opened his presents, Michael announced he had to leave.

Good. Derrick slid a glance to the front door where Allie stood with Maynard. He'd like to speak with Maynard alone someday, grab him by his scrawny neck for hurting Allie.

No. That was the old Derrick. God had been working on his heart, and He was faithful to finish the good work He'd started in him. Plus, who was he to judge Maynard? Derrick hadn't been exactly up-front.

An hour later, everyone else had left. Danny tugged on his shirtsleeve. "Mr. Derrick! Can you stay and watch me play the game you gave me?"

"Did you ask Aunt Allie and Granny if it would be okay?"

Danny waved his hand. "Of course it's okay. They don't care about stuff like that."

"You sure?" Derrick laughed. Danny had the run of the house for sure. He followed the boy into the den.

Danny settled beside him on the sofa, his thumbs already working the handheld game system controls. "My friends have this game. It's awesome. Thank you."

Derrick wished more than anything he could sit with Danny like this every night. After only a few minutes, Danny yawned. "I'm tired, Mr. Derrick." He swiped his eyes.

"Me, too." Derrick tapped him on the shoulder. "Did you have a good birthday?"

"Yeah. Really good, but. . ." Danny coughed, got up, and went to the bookcase. "I miss my. . ."

"What's wrong, Spiderman?" Derrick moved to the end of the sofa cushion. "You crying?"

Danny shrugged, swiped his hand across his eyes, then pulled an album from the shelf. "This is my first birthday without my mom and dad."

Yes, of course. The thought hadn't crossed Derrick's mind. "I'm sorry, Danny. Do you need to talk about them?"

Danny shrugged again. "Not much to say, really. They're dead. I know I'll see them again in heaven, but sometimes I miss them a lot. I want a mom and dad."

He studied his precious nephew, at a loss for words. What could he say to such raw emotion?

Danny opened the album and pointed to a photo. "This is them and me. Last year."

"Look at you on that roller coaster!" Derrick fake punched Danny in the shoulder. "Even I'm scared to go on those big rides."

Laughing through his tears, Danny punched Derrick back, and Derrick wrapped his arm around the boy's thin shoulders. "You're a chicken," Danny hiccuped. "I thought heroes were never chickens."

"Every hero has at least one flaw. Remember that." His heart broke for Danny's pain. "And your parents looked like a happy couple. You must've had lots of fun with them."

Danny wiped the tears off his cheeks, leaving wet smudges on his face. "At least I have my granny and Aunt Allie." He smiled despite his tears. "She's the best aunt in the whole world. She loves me, and she's not afraid of big rides."

"She'd make a great superhero, too," Derrick said.

"Yeah."

"I know she loves you. You're easy to love, Danny." Derrick released a pent-up breath. "But if she's not afraid of big rides, maybe you shouldn't tell her I'm a chicken. Heroes don't like to talk about their flaws."

"Scout's honor." Danny closed the album. "I think I'll go upstairs now. Thank you for the present." He crossed the room, turned back, and hugged Derrick, who felt his own eyes burn.

"Mr. Derrick," Danny said, "will I see you tomorrow?"

"I don't know if I'll be back." Derrick's heart pounded. What was the point of getting closer to this family? He was falling hard for Allie. Betsy Vahn felt like a second mother to him. And Danny... His nephew had stolen a chunk of his heart.

Danny backed away, and his smile faded. "Okay then, see you sometime." He walked from the room, head down.

The boy was getting too attached. *Lord, I've been completely self-centered*. He hadn't considered Danny's emotions before barging into the Vahns' lives. The poor kid didn't need anyone else to depart from his life. And even if Derrick spent more time here, sooner or later he'd have to return home. His facade couldn't continue indefinitely.

The time had come to leave Walla Walla. Tomorrow he would take Allie to Bright's like she suggested, then he'd return home and handle everything else by telephone and fax. No need to continue here.

He stood, stretched his legs, then headed to the kitchen to say good-bye to everyone. But before he could enter the room, he heard Betsy's voice.

"Allie, you mustn't overreact. I'm sure there's a reasonable explanation."

"This explains the debt he left, Ma. At least we know that much."

He heard the sound of a chair scraping on the floor. "I need to see what Derrick and Danny are up to. We'll talk more tomorrow."

Derrick was about to be caught eavesdropping. He hurried back into the family room and turned toward the bay window.

"Where's Danny?" Allie asked behind him.

"He's gone to bed." Derrick turned toward her. He needed

to tell her about the photo album and Danny's tears, but not with the deep pain already etched on her face.

"Are we still on for tomorrow?" *Please say yes.*

Allie nodded. "Yes, of course."

Derrick smiled, reached out to give her a hug, but dropped his arms at his sides. Unless he could tell her the whole truth and nothing but, he didn't deserve Allie's affection.

fourteen

As he took Allie's hand to guide her into the truck, Derrick caught another whiff of her flowery perfume, reminding him of their kiss—a distraction he didn't need. He'd have to work hard to keep his wits about him today. Squelch the urge to kiss her at all costs.

He closed the door, came around to the driver's side, and started the engine. He wracked his brain to think of something to talk about so he wouldn't slip and say, *Hey, I know what I said about being friends, but I really liked that kiss yesterday. Could we try again?* Or, *Did you know you're Danny's aunt, but I'm his uncle? And may I kiss you again?* And then there was the conversation he'd overheard last night. *Hey, Allie. Not only am I not telling you that I'm Danny's uncle, I also eavesdropped on you. What's up with the debt?*

"So, I take it from the frogs I hear at night that the road is named Frog Hollow for a reason?"

"Oh yeah." Allie smiled. "I used to love trying to catch them at the pond."

Talk of the pond brought back a rush of fresh memories of their kiss. Derrick searched his mind for a change of topic. "I bet Danny enjoys frog hunting, too."

"That and picnics near the pond." Allie sighed. "I guess all that will have to end soon."

Poor Allie. She was suffering having to give up the land. That they would still have their house and a few acres wouldn't make things easier. She'd probably die a little bit with each house a developer built on the land she used to ride on. This was one time he hated his job. Maybe he could send her money anonymously. With everything in him, he wanted to do something to help the Vahns. Still, that wouldn't help them keep all their land.

"You can make a left here. I'm taking you to town a different way." Allie smiled at him with genuine warmth. If she had a clue as to why he'd come to Walla Walla, she wouldn't be friendly. Guilt washed over him. How had a simple search for his nephew become ugly and complicated?

Derrick hit the turn signal. "I've never taken this road." But he was willing to go wherever Allie wanted to take him.

"This is mostly farmland, but if you get bored—"

"No, I won't get bored." *Not with you sitting beside me.*

"Good." She settled back against the seat then turned toward him, her gaze glued to his face. Did she see the strong resemblance between himself and Danny? Derrick cleared his throat. It was dangerous for him to be alone with her. A part of him wanted to spill every secret—confide his purpose for coming to Walla Walla. But he did owe her one truth right now.

"About Danny, I think you should know that he showed me a photo album last night. Pictures of him and his folks. He said this was his first birthday without them." Derrick choked up, took a breath, and started again. "The kid was crying. I tried to cheer him—"

"Oh no." Allie's face lost color. "My poor little boy."

"I'm sorry." Derrick reached over and squeezed her hand. "I didn't mean to upset you."

"I'm glad you told me." Allie squeezed his hand in return. "My sister-in-law, Cindy, started the album as soon as she and Luke adopted Danny." She sniffed. "I can't believe it most days. None of this is real."

"I've got tissues in the glove compartment."

Allie released his hand and snapped it open. "Thanks."

"Does Danny know he's adopted?"

Allie nodded. "Yes, Cindy and Luke felt they owed Danny the truth. They let him know as soon as he could understand. They told him he was special, handpicked by God for them."

He felt Allie shutting down, but he needed more answers. "Sounds like Cindy and Luke were thrilled to get Danny."

"Oh, Cindy would only allow me to hold Danny long enough for her to take a shower." Allie laughed, and he loved the musical sound of it. "Luke and Cindy, they were a dynamic couple. So in love and happy." She glanced out the side window as though a new thought had stolen her attention. "At least most of the time, but at the end. . ."

Derrick held his breath, waiting. But as the seconds ticked by, he accepted that Allie had clammed up on the topic and he'd get no more from her. Pain was like that. You just had to shut it out sometimes.

Allie sat forward and pointed. "Did you know the Nez Perce Trail was located right here on Main Street?"

"No. Maybe I should brush up on Walla Walla's history since I live nearby in the Tri-Cities."

"My dad was a history buff, and I spent many Saturdays with him exploring this area. His research files fill a whole drawer in the cabinet in my office. I haven't had the heart to look at them until yesterday." She balled the frayed tissue in her hand. "He once talked about writing a book."

"No kidding?" The sadness in her voice cut him to the core. Time for a change of topic. "I do know that Walla Walla means 'place of many waters.'"

"Yep." She smiled. "Good job. See? You do know something."

"A bit. But I'd like to learn more from you."

"My pleasure."

Allie showed him all her favorite places in town, giving him a litany of history. A tour guide couldn't have done better. They finally parked near Bright's Candies.

"Weird, being here with you."

Worry wormed its way into his heart. "Why's that?"

"This is where we met for the first time."

Relief relaxed his stiff shoulders. As if he could ever forget. "You mean when you knocked my whole bag of jelly beans to the ground?"

She laughed. "At the time you said it was fine. Now you're changing your story?"

"Never." He squeezed her shoulder. "You're fast becoming one of my favorite people on the planet."

Smiling, Allie tilted her head. "That's sweet. Do you really mean it?"

He thought about what he'd blurted out, and yes, it had come from the heart. "I mean it." Derrick hopped out of the truck and walked around to her side before he did something stupid.

He opened the door for her, took her hand, and helped her out of the car. Not that she needed his help. She'd demonstrated physical and emotional strength he wasn't sure he possessed. She'd held up after her dad, sister-in-law, and brother died. Would he have that strength when Sandy passed away?

They entered Bright's, and he abandoned his morbid thoughts and instead inhaled deeply of the sweet scent that hung in the air. The mixture of chocolate and sugar. . .and Allie by his side. What more could a man ask for?

"Yum, what should we get?" Allie stood in front of the counter smiling.

Derrick eyed the goodies behind the glass, licked his lips, and pointed. "Fudge."

"I take it you like fudge?"

"Love it." He patted his well-toned stomach as if that was proof enough. "How about you?"

"I like their mint truffles." She looked relaxed now. Maybe he'd scaled the walls around her heart. Then again, maybe it was Bright's atmosphere. Everybody turned into a kid when entering a candy store.

After they ordered, they sat outside at a table in the sunshine and shared their sweets. "This was a good day, Allie. Thanks for taking the time."

"Uh-uh. No need to thank me. I should be thanking you. I haven't done anything for fun in far too long."

"That explains it then." Derrick pointed at her face.

"What?" Allie laughed. "What are you grinning about?"

"Can't take you anywhere." Squinting, he leaned forward. "You've got chocolate on your cheek."

"Do I?" She wiped her face with her fingers. "Did I get it?"

He shook his head, then picked up his napkin, reached across the table, and wiped the corner of her mouth.

Allie remained stone still. The look in her eyes made his heart beat faster. If they weren't in public, he would've kissed her again. "I guess we should—"

"Yes, let's go." Allie gathered their candy wrappers and tossed them in the trash.

He had to stop sending her mixed signals. Unless, and until, Sandy gave him permission to identify himself as Danny's uncle, their relationship didn't have a chance. And if he was able to admit the truth, Allie might totally reject him for leading her on. He would probably lose no matter what.

They walked to his truck, and his cell phone vibrated. Derrick pulled it from the holder on his belt and glanced at the screen. "My mother. . ." Fear weighted his limbs.

Allie walked a discreet distance from him.

Derrick hit the TALK button. "Mom?"

"Derrick, Sandy has taken a turn for the worse. They say it won't be long."

fifteen

Early Monday morning a blaring alarm clock startled Allie awake. Grumpy from fitful sleep, she slapped the OFF button, then stomped to the bathroom to get ready for the day. She had an early appointment to shoe an Arabian gelding nicknamed Goober. The name suited him. His markings and classic Arabian looks made him appear regal and distant, but only because he was too dumb to act any other way.

Scrubbing her face, she told herself it could be worse. She could be returning to work on Eddieboy, who was smart enough to pretend he was dumb before lashing out with his teeth.

In the kitchen her mood didn't improve when her favorite coffee cup shattered onto the floor, victim of her half-closed eyes and errant elbow.

What was yesterday about? Why had she been so silly to ask Derrick to go to Bright's? Why had he accepted? Derrick's quick end to their day in Walla Walla only compounded her confusion. She knew his mother called and there had been a family emergency, but she didn't know what it was. She had locked lips with a total stranger. But still, the ugly reminder emerged—knowing a person a long time meant nothing, either. She'd grown up with Luke. She'd looked up to him as her older brother, yet she'd discovered he'd been deceiving her for years and maybe his wife, Cindy, as well. Why all the checks to Paige?

Allie stared at the shards of ceramic on the floor. That's what her life felt like. As if a big hand had picked her up, dropped her, and pieces of her emotions were scattered all over.

She went to the utility closet and grabbed the broom. Once

again since Pastor's prayer for her, she longed for a return to the kind of faith that would make her want to open her Bible first thing in the morning, meditate on the scripture, and get on her knees for a conversation with God. To return to the faith she'd drifted away from, captured by the cares of this world and her own resentments. It seemed a long way back.

❧

Two hours later, after her session with Goober, Allie stopped by the coffee shop in town. She sat at a small round table next to the window, ordered a skinny latte with two extra shots of espresso, and stared outside. If only she could turn off her brain for a while—forgive and forget and get rid of the anger. Her mental churning made her head ache and her heart pound.

The young waitress, looking as carefree as a summer breeze, brought her the latte. Allie nodded and smiled a thank-you. Not so long ago she was as cheery as the server. That's when Dad was strong and full of life. And Luke and Cindy may have had their battles, but when they'd sneak peeks at one another across the table, they appeared madly in love.

Or was it all an illusion? Could anybody truly know another person? Allie sipped her drink and gazed out the window again. An older couple shuffled along the sidewalk, hand in hand. How sweet. Romantic. She closed her eyes and saw only one man with whom she'd love to grow old. A man she might never see again.

She opened her eyes, and the dream disappeared. Was that Paige Maynard crossing the street? Allie gritted her teeth. Just look at her! Perfectly groomed. Dressed to the nines. Were her clothes bought with Luke's money while she and Ma had to sell off their land to pay off Luke's company credit cards?

Allie stood and tossed her empty cup in the garbage, her throat suddenly dry. Despite a little voice in the back of her head telling her to take a deep breath and calm down, she threw open the door, charged across the street, and met a startled Paige on the sidewalk.

"Allie." Paige took a step back. "Wh-what's wrong?"

"We need to talk."

"Uh, what about?" Paige glanced around, and her gaze slid back to Allie. "Is this about Danny's adoption?"

Allie blinked. "Danny's adoption?" Ah, the parade. Understanding dawned. "I wouldn't use you as my attorney if I decide to adopt Danny, if that's what you're asking."

"Oh. . .that's fine, of course." Paige's shoulders sagged. "Still, I could do the paperwork. I handled the first adoption." She motioned toward the coffee shop. "Do you want to go inside and grab a cup of coffee with me?"

"No, I don't want anybody to overhear." Allie pointed to the park bench across the street. "We're going to need privacy and time."

Paige drew a deep breath. Did she know what was coming?

"Of course. I've always got time for you, Allie"

Allie stepped off the curb, and Paige followed. Something was very, very wrong here. Paige was too compliant and overfriendly. Must be the guilt.

They sat, and Allie looked her dead in the eyes. What had Luke seen in this woman? All the makeup. The opposite of Cindy with her natural beauty.

"I think you know what this is about," Allie blurted and took pleasure in the sight of Paige's guilty face going white.

"You look angry, and I don't even know what I've done." Paige's voice broke off. "At least give me a hint of what we're talking about here."

Allie snorted a humorless laugh. "All right, if you want to play stupid I'll spell it out for you. Hint number one: I found my brother's check stubs. That ring a bell?"

Paige shook her head. "I don't understand."

"Of course you don't." Allie scanned the expensive designer clothes, and fury rose up in her to a level she'd never known. "I'm going to warn you that I won't abide lying, Paige. I'll have more respect for you if you fess up and be a woman about this."

Nodding, Paige licked her lips. "Yes, Luke gave me money—"

"Because you and my brother were having an affair, right?"

Paige pressed two manicured fingernails to her frosted pink lips. Her gaze darted left and right before she blew out a long breath. "Can you ever forgive me, Allie?"

"No!" Allie's nails bit into her palms. "You knew he was married with a son." She choked up. It was true after all. The money worries slipped from her mind along with the anger, replaced by memories of Luke and overwhelming sadness. "Why you?"

Paige flinched like she'd been slapped. "It was wrong, I admit, but you don't have to be vicious." She shot to her feet. "We were in love. We had been for years, you know. Since high school."

"When people are in love"—Allie stood and came within an inch of her face—"it doesn't require an exchange of money."

"There was the rent on my apartment." Paige had the decency to look down at the sidewalk. "We needed a place to meet."

"A place to meet?" Bile rose at the back of Allie's throat. No wonder Paige had moved out of her father's mansion. "And you're trying to tell me *you* don't have money of your own with that wealthy family of yours?"

Paige shrugged. "Daddy is stingy, you know. I get my paycheck from the law firm, of course, but I needed more." She sniffled. "I loved Luke. It wasn't easy for me, either, carrying this secret."

"A secret?" Allie snapped. "That's not what I'd call it. Adultery is more like it."

"Please." Paige reached her hands out in supplication. "What are you going to do?"

Allie ignored the gesture and backed away. "I have no idea what I'm going to do." She whirled around and took long strides toward her truck. She looked over her shoulder and couldn't resist one last jab. "What do you think your father would do if he found out?"

"You wouldn't tell him, would you?" Paige's face was ash white.

Allie took no pity on her and didn't wait for a response. She pulled open the truck door, jumped inside, and turned the key. As she drove away, she burst into tears.

❧

Derrick forked pieces of stuffed french toast around his plate, trying to force himself to eat. Last thing he wanted was to hurt Hank's feelings since the chef had prepared one of Derrick's breakfast favorites, as he'd done for the rest of the family this morning. Hank had faithfully served the Owenses for nearly two decades and took part in raising him and Sandy. Cooking was Hank's remedy for the bad things in life. When Sandy broke up with boyfriends, he cajoled smiles from her with her favorite oatmeal chocolate chip cookies. Derrick's broken arm in grade school was treated with a large dose of snickerdoodles. Hank handled pain by cooking, whether it was his own or someone else's. And today he was trying to fix everybody's grief with his delicious creations.

He was scrubbing the already spotless dark granite counter. Pots hung from hooks, their copper bottoms gleaming like new pennies. Hank kept a tidy kitchen, but today every inch of the room sparkled. Derrick wished he had the energy to work out his grief with something productive. Instead it was as if he were paralyzed. He could think of nothing else but Sandy lying in her bed upstairs, the hospice nurse by her side. Her lucid moments had diminished, and he understood why his parents were maintaining their vigil anywhere but in his sister's room. No words could express the pain of watching a loved one pass away from this world.

"It's okay. You don't have to eat." Hank dropped on a stool opposite him at the kitchen island.

Derrick looked up. Buried in thought, he hadn't noticed

Hank walk across the kitchen. "Sorry. Any other day I would've devoured—"

"I understand, believe me." Hank blinked back tears. "Hard to let go of our little girl."

Feeling like a kid, Derrick wiped his nose with a napkin and stood. "I need to go be with her."

"Of course." Hank reached across the island and rested his hand on his shoulder. "I'm here if you get hungry."

As Derrick walked down the hall toward the main staircase, Dad popped his head out of the study. "Derrick, I'd like to speak with you, please."

Derrick sucked in a breath. He needed to see Sandy, but his father's tone demanded compliance.

Dad was ensconced behind his desk. Strain stretched the skin across his face, making it look almost like a mask.

"What's going on with the land in Walla Walla?"

Derrick summoned an all-business tone. "I've got preliminary papers drawn up. I need to get them signed."

"Good. Please stay at it. I may have another developer who's interested in a large piece of property for a new housing development." Dad grinned wolfishly. "We could begin a bidding war."

"That would be good." Now that Derrick had an idea of the extent of the Vahns' debt, he wanted to do everything he could to help them. Perhaps this would bring more money.

Derrick watched his father pull something from his desk. It was the photo Derrick had given to Sandy of Danny and his grandma. A tense silence hung in the room while he heard his pulse pounding in his ears.

"Do you know anything about this?" Dad asked, tapping the photo with his forefinger.

Derrick swallowed hard. Did his father know? "Where did you get that?"

"It fell out of Sandy's Bible." Dad squinted at it. At least the photo wasn't a close-up. He wouldn't be able to see Danny's eyes.

The less said, the better. Derrick waited, holding his breath.

Dad finally looked up. "Must be one of her friends' kids. She was always praying for someone." His harsh tone made it clear what he thought of prayer as a way of seeking answers.

Derrick nodded. He wouldn't have to lie. . .again. "I'm going to sit with Sandy for a while."

His father studied the photo again, and Derrick made a quick escape.

As he stood in the doorway to Sandy's room, Derrick whispered, "God, help me." A memory of Allie infused him with strength. She had lost three family members, but she kept on.

Leanne, the hospice nurse, stood and waved him in.

He tiptoed to Sandy's bed and whispered, "I'll sit with her for a while."

"I'll wait outside in the hall."

When she was gone, Derrick sat, and Sandy opened her eyes. "D-man."

"You're awake?" He reached for her hand.

"I won't be here much longer." She spoke with effort, and tears filled her dark eyes.

"I know." He swallowed, unable to see through the blur of his tears.

"Hey." She squeezed his fingers. "I know for a certainty I'll see you again. Meantime, you're going to be happy."

"Don't talk to me about happiness today." Derrick choked on a sob.

Sandy managed a weak smile. "My only regret is you and Allie."

Derrick wiped at the tears on his cheeks with his fingers. "What?"

"I think you're falling in love with her."

An automatic denial came to his lips. He opened his mouth, closed it, then leaned his weary head against Sandy's bony hand.

"It's true, and I'm standing between you two. I made you hide your identity."

Allie had been in his thoughts constantly, and he'd tried to push her out. He had too much grief to deal with right here in front of his eyes. Knowing he'd left behind a woman he could love with all his heart and a nephew he wanted to help raise made the pain of loss unbearable.

Derrick sat up. "Don't fade away on me, Sandy, please."

"Listen. I was wrong. Tell Allie the truth."

The truth. "I don't think she'll listen."

"Tell her, and send Mom and Dad in here now."

A deep sob ripped through his chest. Derrick leaned down and kissed her cheek. "I love you. I always will."

"I love you, too, Derrick."

He walked out of her room, knowing in his heart he'd never hear her speak those words again, never hear the sound of her laughter.

Tears flooded his eyes as he headed toward the office, but his dad already stood in the hall. "Sandy wants you to come—"

"I'm going to her room now." Dad swiped his hand over his face. "Your mother will join me." He walked past quickly, but not before Derrick saw the tears, the gray pallor of his face.

Leanne put a hand to his arm. "Will you be okay?" She handed him a wad of tissues.

Derrick wiped his eyes and nodded. "I'll be okay, but I'll never be the same."

"Loss does that, but God wants you to go on. Sandy's work here is almost done, but I suspect the good Lord has plenty for you to do yet."

A short laugh escaped his tight throat. "You've been talking to Sandy, haven't you?"

Leanne wrapped her hand around his wrist. "Sandy said to tell you that you *must* invite me to the wedding."

sixteen

"Lord, I'd rather not have known."

Allie headed home and caught herself going over the speed limit. She had to get there before Jake's mom dropped Danny off.

She hated herself for grilling Paige. Instead of fond memories of Luke, she'd forever live with the ugly truth. An adulterer? How could it be so? Nearly every word Luke spoke, every romantic gesture toward Cindy, all of it a lie! Is that the reason Luke gave Paige money—to keep her quiet? "Let it be true, Lord." At least it would mean Luke wasn't in love with Paige. That he only paid her off to keep the truth from Cindy.

As she pulled into the driveway, Allie's hands shook. She saw Jake's mother, Mary, waiting in the car and drew a jagged breath. She wanted to expose Paige for who she was—even to Mary—shout it from the rooftops, but the Vahn family would fall into disgrace as well. Luke was the married man with a son.

"Hey, Allie." Mary pointed at the tire as Allie got out of the truck. "Your tire is low on air."

Allie sighed. One more thing to worry about. "Thanks, and thank you for bringing Danny home. We appreciate it."

"Anytime," Mary said. Danny exited the car and waved good-bye.

After they went inside, Danny headed straight to the fridge. "Aunt Allie, is Mr. Derrick coming over again?"

"Wash your hands before you eat." Poor kid. "I'm really not sure, sweetheart." *But I'd love to know.* "So tell me, how was VBS?"

"Good." Danny shrugged, dried his hands, and returned to the refrigerator. His forlorn look made her face heat with anger all over again. Yet another man in and out of Danny's life. She felt at a loss. Should she speak to him about Derrick? Or about missing his parents on his birthday? Or should she let it go? Maybe he needed more grief counseling. Come to think of it, maybe Allie did, too.

"What are you hunting for in the fridge?" She came up behind him and ruffled his dark hair.

"I don't know." He took out a carton of milk and looked up. "Can you call him? Mr. Derrick, I mean."

"How about I make you a peanut butter and jelly sandwich?"

"Okay, but. . ." Danny wouldn't be sidetracked. He poured himself a tall glass of milk. "Can *I* call him then?"

Now what, Lord? Allie assembled his sandwich. "I don't think you should be calling Mr. Derrick, hon." She cut the crusts off the bread, quartered it, and set the snack in front of him at the table.

"But he likes me." Danny took a hearty bite. "I could tell because—"

"You're talking with food in your mouth again." She grabbed a napkin and brushed at his face the way Derrick had done to her at Bright's. How long before she'd get Derrick out of her mind? "What were you going to say about Mr. Derrick?" *Pathetic!* Pumping her nephew for a few crumbs of information.

"He's fun. He calls me Spiderman, just like you and Granny." Danny's brows scrunched together. Yikes! Did he copy that facial expression from Derrick? She couldn't recall if Danny had ever pulled such a face. "I think he likes you, too." He covered his mouth and giggled. "He looks at you a lot."

"Danny!" Allie's pulse did double-time. "People look at people when they speak." Here she was again, mining for hope. "It's only polite."

He swallowed another bite and shook his head. "He was *staring* at you."

Allie heard the sound of a car in the driveway, jumped up, and went to the window. "Oh, Granny is home." All the excitement seeped out of her. She had the heartbreaking task of having to tell her mother what she'd learned from Paige this afternoon.

seventeen

On Tuesday, with his cell phone clutched tight in the palm of his hand, Derrick paced the upstairs hall. His parents had come out of Sandy's room and walked straight past him without a word. A moment later Leanne emerged. One look at her told him no words were necessary.

Sandy was gone—at her going-home party, dancing on streets of gold with Jesus. No more sickness and pain and sorrow.

But what about him?

He ducked into his room, closed the door, and dropped onto a leather sofa. Memories of their youth came rushing back. Sandy the tomboy. How many times had he bandaged her up before his parents got home, hiding that Sandy had done something dangerous—like taking flight with her pogo stick from the high porch? Climbing a tree to the top, hanging upside down, then falling?

"Lucky you've still got a brain," he'd told her. And Sandy quipped, "I'm smarter than you any day, D-man." And she was.

Derrick buried his face in his hands and wept. If only Sandy and Danny could've met, just once.

"Why, Lord?" Derrick stood, slammed his fist against the wall, then drew a breath. He went to the window and pushed aside the curtain. The hearse. They had come for her. He would not see her again until he, too, went to heaven.

❧

Allie zipped her suitcase closed, grabbed the handle, and shut her bedroom door. "Ma?"

"I'm right here, hon." Ma stood at the bottom of the staircase holding two brown bags.

Allie descended the stairs, smiling. Her mom was one of a

kind. "You're sending us off with lunch?"

"Sure, you've got a long ride. In this bag I've got a sandwich for you." She waved her right hand. "This one's for Shannon. Tell her it's that weird, healthy stuff she likes."

"That's sweet." Allie laughed and gave her a hug. "Thanks." She stepped back. "But I still don't know how you and Shannon talked me into this. I'm going to lose a lot of money by not working."

"Tending to the spiritual is far more important for you right now," Ma said as they walked to the front door and Allie pulled it open. "It's only four days. You'll come back refreshed and renewed."

"What if you need me for something? What if there's an emergency? I won't be able to call you. There isn't any wireless or cell phone access on top of that mountain."

"Stop it! There is a phone at the monastery if there's an emergency." Ma gave her a light shove and followed her onto the porch. Then she stopped and pointed. "Oh my, are you going in Shannon's truck? Will that green thing make it?"

"My truck's got a flat, remember?" Allie smiled down at Shannon and waved. "Don't worry, Ma, it's only a three-hour drive."

"I won't worry, I'll pray." She gave her one last hug. "I'll get your flat fixed while you're gone."

With her bright smile, Shannon waved to Ma and blew a kiss.

Allie hurried toward the truck before she had a chance to change her mind. Three days. No communication.

She opened the rusted back door, and the tired hinges moaned a protest. Would the truck make it there and back? Allie sighed and tossed her suitcase atop a mess of random items.

"Isn't this exciting?" Shannon asked.

"Um. . ." Allie hopped into the passenger seat, set down the lunch bags and her purse, and shrugged. "I'm kind of worried that we'll be incommunicado for four days."

"Of course you're worried." Shannon pulled away from the curb, smiling. "You're Allie."

"Hmm." She couldn't argue the point. Shannon knew her too well. "Question. How will you *not* talk for hours everyday?"

"You know, I asked myself that very same question." A serious expression crossed her face. "But Ray—I'm talking to him about taking guitar lessons when I move to the Tri-Cities—he told me the atmosphere in a monastery is so sacred I won't want to disturb the peace."

"So, this Ray—sounds like he knows you well." Allie laughed. "Any romantic interest?"

"No-o-o." Shannon wagged her head. "He's another—"

"Friend." Allie finished the sentence for her and sighed. "I envy you that. Michael started out as my friend, ended up a boyfriend, and now I avoid him like the plague. I guess I can't handle the friend thing with a guy, especially one I've dated."

"No way you could be friends with Michael now." Shannon turned onto Highway 11 toward Pendleton, Oregon. "He's jealous of Derrick. I saw that right away at Danny's party."

"I don't know why he'd be jealous of Derrick. It was over between Michael and me long before Derrick was in the picture."

"Aha! So he *is* in the picture."

A sinking feeling hit the pit of her stomach. "No. It's more like Derrick walked off into the sunset and disappeared. He hasn't phoned, even about the property." Allie snapped her fingers. "Gone. Just like that."

"Doesn't sound like Derrick." Shannon slid her gaze her way. "You're falling in love with him, aren't you?"

"No!" Allie's breath caught in her lungs. "I heeded your advice about slowing down. Now everything is at a standstill, and I think it's best I stay away from him."

"That's not what I told you to do! I told you to take it slow, that I felt there was more to Derrick than meets the eye."

"Apparently you were right." Allie gave a nonchalant shrug.

"I haven't heard from him since Sunday." She stared out the side window and sighed. "Not that I care, but he came into Danny's life, and Danny misses him."

"You don't care?" Shannon waved her index finger. "And before you bear false witness, remember that we're going on a monastic retreat."

Allie couldn't suppress a burst of laughter. "What if I do care? Derrick *doesn't*."

"Yeah, sure he doesn't." Shannon smirked. "Something must've happened for him not to call. When we get back home, why don't you call the real estate office?"

"No way." Allie shook her head. "When Michael pulled his disappearing act, I did the calling, innocent that I was. I ended up finding him with that other woman. I've decided if a man is interested, he can pursue me."

"Michael was engaged to you. Derrick isn't obligated."

"Exactly." In her mind's eye, Allie saw Paige and her brother together and shuddered. "For all I know, Derrick Owens could be married."

"Uh-uh." Shannon wagged her head. "No way is Derrick married. I would've picked up on that." She sighed and looked thoughtful for a moment. "But there is something; I just can't pinpoint what he's hiding." She placed her hand over her heart. "I feel it in here."

Allie couldn't take another second of this conversation. Why waste time analyzing a relationship that didn't exist? "Ma packed you a lunch." She tapped the brown bag. "That crazy food you like to eat. Probably bean sprouts and hummus with fried tofu or something."

Shannon laughed. "Not quite, but she's a darling. She knows what I like." Her expression suddenly grew serious. "And don't think I'm not aware that you intentionally changed the subject."

Allie nodded. "I think we can both use this retreat."

Perhaps she'd be able to forgive Paige and Luke and. . .

Please, Lord, help me put Derrick out of my mind, too.

eighteen

By midday Thursday the last of the funeral guests were gone, and the temporary staff had finished cleaning up the dining room where Mom and Dad had graciously received condolences from their friends as well as Sandy's. Derrick now stood alone in the kitchen with Hank, who stared out the window over the sink.

"The service was nice," Hank murmured.

"Yes," Derrick said. "Pastor Clark gave a wonderful message."

Hank turned and leaned back against the counter. "It was exactly what she wanted. So many people got up to speak about her. It was a celebration of her life."

"I'm having trouble celebrating," Derrick said softly.

"I know. Me, too."

"The only thing that helps is knowing her pain is over. But I still want to ask God why. She had such a hard life, and when she finally got it all together, this happens."

Hank nodded. "I gotta admit I have the same questions."

"Life will never be the same." Derrick pulled out a stool and sat at the island.

"You got that right." Hank joined him and rested his hands on the granite. "Kinda makes you think about the future, too, doesn't it? Like maybe we should grab it by the horns and just go for it. Be real. Take chances for love. Not hold back."

"Hank, you're not thinking of anyone in particular, are you?"

The big man who had always been in charge of himself, his emotions, his kitchen, blushed.

Derrick grinned. "That's what I thought. A certain nurse named Leanne would be my guess."

"I'm not saying."

"Yeah, you don't need to." Derrick sighed. "I always thought that's what I was doing. Taking life by the horns. Living day to day. But I wasn't loving. I used people. I didn't know what love really was until I met the Lord."

The two sat quietly for several minutes, then Hank broke the silence. "It's going to be quiet around here, I think. Too quiet. I don't imagine you'll be living in the guest cottage much longer. I need someone to care for." He went to the massive stainless steel refrigerator and peered at the leftovers. "I didn't have an appetite before, but now I'm getting it back." He glanced over his shoulder. "How about you?"

Derrick nodded. "Yeah, the knots in my stomach are starting to come undone."

"Your sister would have wanted us to enjoy the food. You know how she liked to eat. Especially things like this." He took a package from the fridge and brought it to the island.

Derrick leaned forward. "Spring rolls? Philadelphia rolls? I didn't see these earlier."

"I didn't put them out earlier. I hoped we'd have a chance to talk, and I know how much you like them and how much she liked them. It'll be our little celebration." He retrieved some paper towels and gave Derrick two. "One for your plate, the other for hands. Totally informal. For her."

"Sandy was a fireball, wasn't she?"

"Yes, and if she can hear us now, she's having a good laugh." Hank stopped cleaning and looked him in the eye. "I'm sure you already know, but Sandy loved you with her whole heart and soul."

Nodding, Derrick swallowed past the dryness in his throat. "I know, Sandy always wanted the best for me, and near the end she gave me guidance." He couldn't tell Hank all that lay on his heart. "I'm going to heed her advice."

"Is this about her son?"

Derrick felt the blood drain from his face. "How do you know? Does my father know?"

"I don't think your dad knows, but Sandy called me to her room the day before she passed away." Hank's watery gaze searched his face. "Your secrets are safe with me."

"I don't doubt that for a second." Derrick took a deep breath. "But if Sandy told you, do you think she mentioned anything to Mom and Dad?" Worry stirred in the pit of his stomach. Sandy had wanted Derrick to tell Allie the truth. *But what if Dad beats me to the punch?* Dad, short on patience and long on agenda, might contact the Vahns first. Knowing his father, he might even threaten to take Danny. Without an opportunity for Derrick to explain himself to Allie, she'd believe he was an outright liar.

🙚

For the third time Thursday evening, Derrick dialed Allie's cell, only to hear an automatic message. Why would she have shut off her phone? Maybe she was out shoeing horses. He snapped off his phone without leaving a message, then dialed their landline.

"Hello?" Betsy picked up on the first ring.

"Hi, Betsy, this is—"

"Derrick! How are you, and where've you been?" There was a smile in her voice, and it hit hard how much trust she'd put in him.

"My sister passed away," he said. "The funeral was today." Sandy's death registered anew, bringing with it a tidal wave of raw emotion.

"Oh, Derrick. . ." A long silence ensued. He heard her sniff and thanked God again that Sandy's son belonged to a sensitive, caring family. "I don't know what else to say except I'm sorry."

"Thank you." Derrick's eyes burned. Would the tears ever stop? "I know you've been through your own losses."

"Yes, too many." Betsy's voice cracked. "I'd tell Allie to call you back, but she won't be home until Saturday."

"Away." A myriad of thoughts darted through his mind. Where'd she go and with who?

"She's with Shannon at a retreat in a monastery."

"Um, a monastery, you said?" Derrick frowned. The way his

luck was running, Allie would become a nun.

"Yes, it's lovely. I've been there once. Peace and quiet and meditating on God's Word. Thing is, no talking allowed, so she's keeping her phone turned off. Besides, they can't get a cell signal up in the mountains."

Now there was an interesting concept. Overprotective Allie with no cell phone, unable to check for messages from Danny. Exhaustion fell on him like a wet blanket. He needed to get it all out there, tell her the truth. "So I guess I won't be able to speak with her until Saturday."

"Yes, she'll be back in the afternoon." She paused. "Do you have questions about the land? Is this an emergency? Or did you want to tell her about your sister?"

The land was the furthest thing from his mind. "No emergency. And it's not about the land, either. I did want to tell her about my sister." There he went again, avoiding the truth. Yes, he wanted Allie to know about Sandy, but that was not his priority.

"Hang on for a moment, please, Derrick."

He heard Danny's voice in the background.

Betsy inhaled. "Derrick, I must go. And again, I'm sorry. I'll have Allie call you the second she gets in."

"I would appreciate that—" She'd already hung up. Danny must have gotten into some kind of mischief she had to straighten out.

Derrick clipped his cell back to the holder on his waist and turned to see his father in the doorway. How much had he overheard?

nineteen

As Shannon rounded the corner onto Frog Hollow Road, Allie smiled. "There's no place like home."

"True," Shannon said. "But the time away was worth it. I can't believe it's just Saturday. I feel like I've had a month's worth of weekends. I feel renewed and invigorated."

"Absolutely. I feel like I'm ready for anything now. Like I can face the giants." Allie dug into her purse and pulled out her cell. "I have no voice mails. I assume everything is okay at home. And then there is that one voice mail from Derrick just saying hello. He said I didn't have to call back, so I'm not going to."

"You could, you know."

"I don't have to, you know."

Shannon laughed. "Playing hard to get will just attract him more."

"Great," Allie said. "I spent the last few days keeping my mind on the spiritual. I don't need to start thinking about him again."

"I don't think he's going away," Shannon said.

Allie ignored that. "I can't wait to see Danny and Ma. I felt a bit guilty about leaving her alone to care for Danny."

"She said she was going to take Danny to work with her on some days. I bet your mom sold more at my shop than I ever did. She's so good with the customers."

"Yes. She's just great with people." Allie noticed a fast-food restaurant.

"Hey, I'm starving," Shannon said. "You want to stop?"

"How about I make us something at home?" Allie smiled.

"I know." Shannon flashed her a grin. "You just want to get home to see Danny."

"You got it." Allie eyed her house in the distance.

Shannon slowed the truck and turned onto the long drive. "I prayed a lot for you while we were there. And I prayed that something would happen so you wouldn't have to sell any land."

Allie had told Shannon everything on the way to the retreat. Paige, Luke, the checks.

"I prayed about that, too." She glanced at Shannon and shrugged. "It just seems impossible. Though some people might not think the debt Luke left is that bad, he wrote checks against our business credit card accounts. Add interest on top of the amount owed, and I'm not making the minimum payments."

"I know," Shannon said. "But God does miracles."

"Yes, and there's been a minor miracle in me. I prayed that your new business would succeed, and I wouldn't be so selfish about missing you. I prayed and meant it from the heart."

"An hour trip back and forth isn't bad. We can still have our Scrabble nights."

"Yes, we can." But with so many things changing, Allie wondered what the future was going to hold.

As they pulled up to the house, Danny ran out the front door to greet them, a broad smile on his face and his arm in a sling.

"Guess what, Aunt Allie? I broke my arm."

❧

Derrick's mom darted about the reception office of Owens Realty, her pasty face swollen. Derrick had no doubt she was crying in the night. The stately woman who'd worked beside Dad for the past thirty-five years had become a shadow of the vibrant woman she'd once been. He wondered if Sandy's death had marked him, too.

"Sorry to interrupt," he said, "but where's Dad? He left me a list of things to do, including going by the mortgage company to drop off some papers. I have a question, and he's not answering his cell."

"Your father?" She set down a stack of files on the sleek reception desk. "He mentioned something about the Kents. . . buying land in. . .oh, I don't know. I'm trying to straighten up, keep my mind occupied before I lose it."

How could Derrick be such a clod? "Mom." He went to her side, leaned down, and gave her a hug. "I'm sorry. I understand."

"No more Sandy." She sagged against his shoulder and sobbed. A first. He'd never seen her cry, and it tore at his heart. "Your kids are never supposed to go before you."

Derrick wrapped his arms around her and held her for a moment. When she finally pulled away, he tried to figure out a way to ask if Sandy had confessed to them about Danny. "Mom?"

"Yes?" she murmured.

"Did Sandy give you or Dad any last minute requests?"

"Like what?" Mom stepped back and blinked. "Sandy could barely speak. Did you say you're going to the accountant?"

"No, the mortgage company." Her series of questions caught him off guard. The past few days it seemed her thoughts followed no pattern, which added to his worry. All Mom needed was the shock of hearing she had a grandson—or did she already know?

Derrick searched his mother's eyes carefully for any clue that Sandy might've made a deathbed confession, but there were no signs.

"So you don't know where Dad is?"

She perked up just slightly. "Since when has your father ever given me a detailed account of his whereabouts?"

Had Mom taken issue with his dad's long absences throughout the years like Sandy and himself? If she had, she'd kept it well hidden and stood by Dad's side through every crisis and every business deal with never a complaint. She fanned her face and sighed. "Just the Kents, that's all I remember."

"Okay." Uneasiness still plagued him. If Sandy told Hank,

would she have told someone else? Especially if she was under the influence of pain medication? He didn't want to imagine his father driving to Walla Walla and intimidating the Vahns.

Derrick kissed his mom on the cheek. He had to see Allie. "Will you be all right?"

"Yes, of course. I'm going through these files. The work distracts me." She smiled through her tears. "I've been around Hank too long."

Derrick shot out of the office and hurried to his car. He'd get to Allie and calmly explain all. He could only pray she'd give him a chance after that. She made it obvious on more than one occasion that she couldn't abide lying, but maybe she'd find it in her heart to forgive him for avoiding the truth. Because of Sandy.

He stuck the key in the ignition of his Silverado, and it roared to life. As he pulled onto the street toward the mortgage company, he yanked his cell phone from his belt, dialed Allie's number, and waited.

"Derrick!" Allie said after he greeted her. His heart sank at her panicked tone. Did she know? "Ma told me about your sister. I'm so sorry."

Relief. "Thank you," he said. "I know you understand."

"I do."

Derrick wanted to blurt out everything right then and there, but he couldn't. They needed to be face-to-face.

"Oh, if you're coming, you need to know. Danny broke his arm," she said. "I feel like it's my fault. I was away and left all the responsibility to Ma."

"How did he break his arm? Is he okay?" Worry twisted his stomach. He hadn't been there for Danny, either.

"Well, he's fine." Allie paused. "He fell out of a tree. That's my fault, too."

"Why?" Derrick drove toward the mortgage company as fast as the speed limit allowed.

"I taught him to climb that tree, and he was playing Spiderman."

Derrick couldn't help himself. He chuckled.

"I'm not sure it's funny," Allie said, but he could tell she was smiling.

"You know how I got my scar?"

"How?"

"I fell out of a tree playing a superhero."

After a moment's pause, Allie laughed. "You understand then."

"Absolutely. All young boys can fly."

"So. . .you called for a reason, right?" The laughter in her voice died.

"Would it be all right if I came by tonight?" Derrick massaged his aching neck. She just had to agree. This couldn't wait another day.

"Um, sure. Is it about our property?"

"No. But we need to talk." No more half-truths.

"Okay then, sure." The tone in Allie's voice made him realize she did care for him, and she'd probably missed the signs that should've told her he'd fallen for her. Too bad he was about to tear up her world.

Derrick pulled into the parking lot. "I have one errand to run, then I'm on my way. I should be there in a little less than two hours, okay?"

"Definitely okay." Allie's voice became muted. "Derrick, I've got to go now, somebody's at the door. See you later."

"Later," he said and fought the fear he couldn't put a name to.

twenty

With her heart pattering pleasantly, Allie stuffed her phone in her pocket and headed for the stairs. Derrick was coming to see her. Not about the property. She couldn't help but feel a shiver of excitement.

Murmurs of voices came from downstairs. Ma had gotten the door; Allie didn't need to bother. She stood in front of her full-length mirror smiling and fluffed her hair. Then Danny came bounding into the room.

"Aunt Allie, there's a man at the door."

She turned toward him. "Who is it?"

"I dunno." Danny stared at her. "Why are you fixing up?"

She smiled. "Just getting ready for—"

"Allie?" Ma's voice came up the stairs. "I think you should come down here."

Why so serious? Allie left the room and descended the stairs, followed by Danny.

Ma stood in the living room, staring up at a tall man with dark hair. The man had his back to her, and Ma motioned her into the room.

"You need me?" Allie picked up her pace.

The man turned. Allie stepped back and stifled a gasp. An older version of Derrick studied her, then clasped his hands behind his back.

"Allie. . ." Ma said. "This is Richard Owens. Derrick's father." His eyes, black like Derrick's, skimmed over her.

"Mr. Derrick has a father?" Danny stood next to Allie.

Richard's gaze flickered to Danny. His eyes warmed, and a tiny smile played in the corner of his mouth. "Yes, Derrick has a father."

"I'm sorry about your daughter," Allie said.

He finally looked at her again, and the semblance of warmth on his face died. "I appreciate the condolences."

"What happened to your arm, son?" Richard asked.

Danny laughed. "I was Spiderman and fell out of the tree. I always climb that tree."

Richard frowned. "I see."

"Are you here about the property?"

"Call me Richard," he said. "And no. I'm not here about the property. That's Derrick's job."

"Then—"

"I should get right to the point." He took a deep breath. "I'm here about Danny."

"Me?" Danny asked, bouncing on the balls of his feet.

Allie rested her hand on her nephew's shoulder. "Danny? Why?" A bad feeling slammed into the pit of her stomach, and she turned to her nephew. "Honey, why don't you go upstairs and wait for me to call you?"

"But Mr. Derrick's father said—"

"Sweetie, listen to Aunt Allie," Ma said. "Please go to your room now."

Danny must have picked up on her urgency. He left the room with no further argument.

Richard's eyes followed Danny with emotion Allie didn't understand. She felt so totally discombobulated. Richard looked like an older version of Derrick, but the resemblance ended there. Except when he looked at Danny, Richard was coldly businesslike. No easy smile, no warmth in his coal black eyes.

"Please sit." Ma pointed to a chair, then she sat on the sofa.

Allie eyed his fine clothing. He reeked of money. She hated feeling like she wanted to apologize for the worn furniture, which had seen its better days, but Richard Owens sank into a chair, seemingly unfazed.

"So what's this about Danny?" Allie sat beside Ma, and fear lodged in her chest, growing with each passing second.

Richard crossed his legs. Even seated informally, his

presence commanded attention. "In her last days when she was under the influence of painkillers, my daughter talked about having a son. After she died, I found photos and paperwork in her belongings, along with phone messages and texts from Derrick confirming the truth of her words. I immediately contacted my attorney."

A chill raised hairs on the back of Allie's neck, and she opened her mouth to speak, but Ma grabbed her hand and squeezed, signaling her to allow Derrick's father to finish.

"The truth of the matter is that Danny is my grandson. Derrick was here to find him."

Allie clapped her hand over her mouth. The room spun. Danny's eyes. . .and Derrick's. The facts came together in a sickening flash of clarity.

"So Derrick didn't come to Walla Walla for land." Her voice shook. She turned to her mom. "He lied to me. . .to us." The words came out in a hoarse whisper.

Richard scowled. "If it brings you any comfort, you're not the only one my son lied to. He told his mother and me he was in town on business, then went about searching for Sandy's son, investigating your family. I don't know what Derrick hoped to accomplish, but—"

Allie jumped to her feet, fists clenched. "Why are you here?"

Richard held out a placating hand, like he was humoring her. "Please sit down. I'll explain."

For a satisfying moment Allie imagined the little pony Eddieboy going after Richard Owens and clamping his eager mouth on the man's arm. She felt the pressure of Ma's hand, and the moment passed. "Sit, sweetheart. This will all work out."

Allie slumped onto the sofa. "Not if they intend to tell Danny his biological mom just died." She glared at Richard. "Danny's been through enough."

Richard sniffed. "Sandy, as well as the rest of my family, has also been through a lot. My daughter died never seeing her son. A son she was coerced into giving up for adoption."

"Coerced?" Allie shut her eyes and sank back onto the sofa. *Don't yell. Don't cry.* She continued to glare at Richard. She would not allow him to intimidate her. "How can you say that? My brother wouldn't have participated in anything questionable." Even as she spoke, she saw the illogic of her words. Luke had been having an affair with Paige, which was questionable to say the least. But. . .hadn't Paige handled the adoption? A formless thought wriggled in the back of her brain, struggling for clarification.

"Richard," Ma said, "even if that were true and your daughter had somehow been coerced, where is this going?"

"And what is it you want?" Allie asked.

"My grandson." He ran his hand down his tie, nodded, and tilted his head. "I'm open to shared custody. Danny is my daughter's son. Possibly the only grandchild I'll ever have."

Allie stared in disbelief. "Shared custody? Why would we agree to that? Danny doesn't even know you."

"He does now. And he knows Derrick."

"I don't think you have a legal leg to stand on, Mr. Owens." Ma's voice was sure and confident, and Allie drew strength from her.

"Danny's adoptive parents were killed in a car accident. He no longer has parents, just a legal guardian." Richard stood and drew back his broad shoulders. "My wife and I and Derrick are family by blood. If you're not agreeable to informal shared custody, we will do this through the courts. If we do that, you risk losing him altogether."

Allie leaped to her feet. Lose Danny? No! Of course they'd fight. But they had barely enough money for necessities lately, let alone legal fees. Frozen to the spot, strength drained out of her and she could only stare up at him.

"We don't want to confuse Danny or hurt him." Ma stood and draped her arm around Allie. "We've nothing to be ashamed of, Mr. Owens. We love him with all our hearts."

"But it seems you're in financial difficulty. My lawyer's investigator discovered that. You're selling off land. Perhaps you can't provide for Danny like we can." Richard's gaze roamed the room. "Nor does it appear he's well supervised based on his broken arm. I could make a case of that. Would you like to reconsider?" Richard crossed his arms over his chest.

"Money doesn't grow happy children." Allie crossed her arms in imitation of his. "We may not have a fat bankbook, but Danny's the happiest kid you'd ever want to meet."

"We probably should consult our own lawyer," Ma said. "In the meantime, I think our discussion is over, Mr. Owens. I'll see you to the door."

Richard's face seemed to sag. "I'm sorry you feel that way. I can find my own way."

They watched as he walked from the room to the front door.

The door closed with a *snap*, and Allie wheeled around to face her mother. "What a nightmare."

"Yes, so it seems." Ma rubbed her temples.

"Should we have agreed to joint custody?"

Ma shook her head. "No. At least not right now. We don't know the truth for a certainty. And we don't know the Owenses. Except Derrick, and now that's in question. I just can't believe he would deliberately deceive us." Ma focused her eyes on her. "Last thing I want is your faith to be hurt more than it already has been."

"It's not your fault." Allie dropped into a chair, dead exhausted. "He played me, too."

"I'm not sure about that," Ma said. "Time will tell. But one thing for sure, they can't take our little boy."

"What if the adoption was illegal? They've got the money. They can hire hotshot attorneys who'll make the case."

"He said coerced, not illegal," Ma said with a slight smile. "If it had been illegal, a man like Richard Owens would have been here guns blazing. Besides, the Lord is in control." She took a deep breath. "I'm going to make cookies and pray."

They both turned when they heard footsteps on the stairs.

"Aunt Allie? Did Mr. Derrick's father leave?"

"Yes, he left." Allie glanced at her mother for guidance.

"I'm going to make a batch of chocolate chip cookies." Ma held her hand out to Danny. "Come and help me."

"Goody!"

"I'm going out to the barn," Allie said.

"Remember who is in control," Ma said over her shoulder as she guided Danny to the kitchen. "We serve a good God."

Allie hated the thoughts that coursed through her head as she walked to the barn. Resentment and anger that flew in so many directions and at so many targets. The Lord, who hadn't promised a rose garden as Ma always said. And there was Luke, the brother she'd looked up to all her life. What had he done? Participated in a questionable adoption? Betrayed his wife? Then there was her own romantic life, if it could even be called that. Michael the cheater and now Derrick the deceiver. Had he really gotten to know her—kissed her—just to get to Danny?

Allie felt the tears start halfway to the barn. Once she was inside, she draped her arms around Pip's neck and let the waterworks flow. The horse stood patiently as he had for so many years. When the tears finally dried, she felt drained of all emotion and went to the storeroom for her shovel and wheelbarrow. Then she retrieved two bales of straw and placed them in the aisle.

Lord, I feel so lost. I'm not in control. I can't do this anymore.

As she scooped a pile of manure from Pip's stall, she heard the barn door squeak. She turned. Derrick's outline was silhouetted in the setting sun.

twenty-one

The second he met Allie's scorching gaze, Derrick's greeting died on his lips.

"What do you want?" She heaved a load of manure into a wheelbarrow, and he could just imagine where she really wanted it flung.

"I talked to your mother. I know my father was here." Derrick slipped his hands into his trouser pockets, heart constricting, remembering the cool greeting he'd gotten from Betsy and the disappointment in her eyes. He'd never felt so shut out in his entire life.

"Yes, he was."

"I'm sorry." He uttered the words, but knew they couldn't begin to express his regret.

"So am I," Allie said.

Derrick took a couple of steps farther into the barn. "Please hear me out."

"No." Allie shook her head. "I don't want to hear you out. I've had enough listening. I want to ask questions."

"Can we sit, then?" Derrick dropped his gaze. He couldn't bear to see the wounded look in her eyes.

With a wave Allie indicated the bales of straw. Once they were seated, she faced him.

She flicked back her long auburn hair, then clasped her hands in her lap. "The only reason we're talking now is so I can get closure. Don't take it as another opportunity to lie."

Sorrow like a dagger stabbed Derrick's heart. He'd honored Sandy's desires, despite his reservations. Now he'd lost everything. But looking back, could he have done anything differently? He spread his hands. "Ask me anything."

"You came to Walla Walla looking for your nephew, right?"

140

"Yes," Derrick said.

"Was everything a lie? All of it?"

He wagged his head slowly. "I didn't lie to you, Allie. I just never told you my original reason for coming to Walla Walla."

"Did you come to town in search of your nephew and pretend to befriend me and Ma—worst of all Danny—just to get your foot in the door and investigate us?"

"At my sister's request, I came to town in search of my nephew, to make sure he was okay. But I didn't set out to befriend you or deceive you. You fell into my life, so to speak. The befriending was real." He leaned toward her. "When I felt myself becoming attached to Danny and Betsy and attracted to you, I made the decision to stay out of your lives. I couldn't allow any of you to become more attached to me. That's why I didn't call you. But when I suspected my father found out, I came to talk to you. I knew how he would react. I can only imagine what that was like."

"You don't have to imagine. I'll tell you." Allie backed away from him, the conviction in her green eyes sure and strong. "He wants joint custody. He said he'd have no problem dragging us through a legal battle to get *his* grandson. He knew, thanks to you, that Danny's adoptive parents were dead."

"Stop," Derrick said. "I know how he came across. I've lived with the man all my life. But you have to believe me. I told him nothing."

Allie stared at him, tears in her eyes.

"I had a good reason for doing what I did," Derrick said.

"I really don't care." Her voice was so small and sad. "I have just one more question. If you hadn't met me the way you did, snatching me off Chester, would you have inserted yourself into our lives?"

"Probably not. I would have tried to find out what I needed to know without bothering you at all." He swallowed. "But if I had met you in other circumstances some other way, some other time, I would have ended up kissing you just like I did."

A long silence stretched between them, and he searched his mind for the right words, but the wall Allie built around her kept him silent. He knew unless God intervened and a miracle happened, the possibility of a relationship with Allie was gone.

"I'm sorry you lost your sister," Allie finally said. "I'm also sorry things turned out the way they did. I don't know what's going to happen now, but I do know that our friendship is broken. I don't think I can trust you."

Derrick's hopes died. He'd lost her.

She shrugged and got to her feet. "I think you'd better leave now."

He stood and stared down at her, remembering their kiss and how she felt in his arms.

"Mr. Derrick?" Danny's voice came from the barn door.

Allie gasped, and Derrick's muscles grew taut. How much had the boy heard?

He strode toward them and looked up into Allie's dazed face.

"Danny." Allie dropped to her knees in front of him. "I thought you were helping Granny make cookies."

"We finished. She thinks I'm in my room, but I wanted to see Mr. Derrick."

Derrick wanted to sink into the floor. Of all his regrets, the worst was hurting Danny.

Danny shuffled his feet. "I heard you talking." He looked up at Derrick, eyes watery. "I don't understand. Why is your father going to take me away?"

Allie glared at Derrick. He grasped Danny's shoulder. "Nobody is going to take you away from your aunt or grandma. This is where you belong."

"But why does he want to?" Danny asked.

"I'll explain in a little while." Allie met Derrick's eyes and nodded toward the door, silently demanding that he leave.

Derrick exited the barn, feeling like he was leaving his

beating heart at Allie's feet on the dirt floor. As he got into his truck, he wondered how he could keep his promise. Could he stop his father? The man was accustomed to getting his way. He'd even made sure Derrick was detained at the office so he wouldn't interfere with his visit to the Vahns'.

His mind turned over all his options. He had to have someone on his side. As he turned onto Frog Hollow Road, he headed for his final destination before he left Walla Walla.

twenty-two

Allie and Danny walked to the house from the barn.

"Is it true? Derrick's father is my grandfather?" Danny frowned and pursed his lips. "Does that mean Mr. Derrick is my father?"

"No, he isn't." Allie felt an urge to slug something. Now she was forced into telling Danny who his real mother was and that she was dead.

"Why did you make Mr. Derrick leave?" Danny looked at her. "He's my friend."

He's more than that, Allie thought bitterly. "Let's wait and talk with Granny, okay?" She walked into the mudroom with her arm wrapped around Danny. Let Derrick, his dad, or anybody else try to take Danny away from them. Over her dead body.

Ma looked up from cleaning the last remnants of baking in the kitchen. "Danny? I thought you were in your room."

"I wanted to see Mr. Derrick."

"He overheard us talking in the barn. Now he wants to know why Derrick's father is his grandfather and. . ." Allie swallowed. Where did she start?

"I see." Ma set down her dishrag and pointed at the kitchen chairs. "Let's sit." She looked across the table at Danny. "You're nine years old now. I know you'll be able to understand what we tell you. Are you ready?"

Danny nodded solemnly, minus his usual rambunctiousness.

As her mom began to talk, Allie's body went rigid. *Lord, please soften the blow. Give Danny peace.*

❧

Thirty minutes later Allie left the kitchen to make a phone call while Danny continued to hammer his grandmother with questions. Amazingly, he didn't seem terribly disturbed. Perhaps because he'd never met Sandy—or maybe because the Lord had actually softened the blow. Danny had become animated, focusing on the fact that Derrick was his "real uncle."

Derrick. She'd begun to trust him. She'd put her faith in love again, but he'd left her faith in ruins. The irony of that thought struck her, and she could hear the Lord whispering, *Your faith should never be in a man, but in Me. No man is perfect. No man ever will be.*

That slowed her thoughts. It was true—no one was perfect, including her. She made plenty of mistakes. And wasn't her anger and resentment and lack of trust in the Lord just as bad as Derrick's sin of omission? He was right. He had never outright lied to her, and he had finally come to her to tell the truth. At least what he knew.

But Allie had more questions. She needed to know if Danny's adoption had really been coerced. And there was one person who probably knew most of the answers. Paige Maynard. She pulled her cell phone from her pocket and walked to the living room, her long strides fueled by anger. Paige—what had she really done? Yet without Paige, would they have Danny? She began to punch numbers into her cell with trembling fingers.

Lord, I need answers.

Allie hit the last digit of Paige's number, held her breath, and listened to the first ring, then the second endless ring. "Lord, please," she whispered, "let her pick up."

"Paige here."

"This is Allie." She drew in a breath. "I had a visitor today. He told us that Danny's adoption had been coerced."

A long silence ensued. "Paige? Are you there? Hello?"

"I don't understand." She spoke in a clipped tone. "Who told you such a lie?"

Allie hesitated a beat. Paige had admitted to the affair with Luke, and what could be worse than that? Yet something in her gut told her to press on. "This person has evidence to the contrary."

"What type of evidence? And who is this person?"

"Richard Owens. The biological mother's father." Allie paced. She wasn't about to show her cards, not without knowledge of all the facts. Her thoughts returned to Luke, the money. She just couldn't accept that her brother had carried on an affair with the likes of Paige—the woman who'd chased him through high school and beyond.

"That money Luke gave you. . ." Her thoughts were a swirl of confusion. Too much had happened today. Allie sent up another silent prayer and started again. "You persuaded a drug-addicted young woman to give up her baby."

"Oh, wait just a second. That's right. Cindy was working in the rehab clinic when Sandra Owens came in pregnant, desperate, and begging for help. *Cindy* did all the talking and made the arrangements. Fine, I drew up the papers, but I'm not going to take the rap for this." Her breath hissed through the phone. "I'm talking to Michael. You'll see. I did nothing wrong. I was helping three people achieve what they wanted."

"Are you trying to tell me you put your reputation on the line for Cindy? I thought you hated her for marrying my brother."

"Well, the adoption was helping him, really. I would've done anything for Luke."

Allie's heart thudded with a sickening thought. "And the money? What was that for? Were you telling the truth when you said Luke had an affair with you?"

"Why would I lie? It's embarrassing enough."

❧

Through the front window of The Quaint Shop, Derrick saw Shannon unpacking a cardboard box. The CLOSED sign hung in the window, but he banged on the front door.

Shannon looked up, dusted off her hands, and smiled warmly while she ran to unlock the door.

"Derrick, nice to see you," she said breathlessly. "I'm so

sorry about your sister."

Allie must not have phoned her yet. "Thank you." He didn't know where to start. "Would you have a couple of minutes to talk?"

"Of course! It's been quiet today." With a wave, she summoned him to the back of the store. "How about I make us some tea?"

"That would be nice." Derrick followed her through the tie-dyed curtains and took the same chair that he'd sat in when he'd last drunk tea with Shannon. When he'd stayed and played Scrabble, sitting next to Allie.

Shannon busied herself filling the pot at the sink.

"I won't beat around the bush. I had an agenda the day of the parade when I walked in here for the first time."

"I knew that." Shannon didn't miss a beat. She set the pot on the burner, lit the pilot light with a strike of a match, then came to sit across from him. "Does Allie know?"

Derrick nodded. "I just left her. She has every right to loathe and distrust me, but I wasn't able to tell her everything. She shut down on me. Wouldn't let me tell her everything."

"She does that," Shannon said.

"I thought maybe if you'll give me a chance to explain, you could talk to Allie. At the very least, it might take some of the pain away."

Shannon took a deep breath and sat back in her chair, studying him with her clear gaze. "I told you I liked you when we first met. I have instincts about people, and how I feel about you hasn't changed. But I can't promise I'll talk to Allie until I hear what you've got to say. I won't manipulate her. She's gone through too much emotional pain already."

"Fair enough." He clamped his hands together on the tabletop and looked into her compassionate hazel eyes. "I'm grateful she has you to lean on because I've added to that pain. For that reason I wish I'd never come to Walla Walla."

"Then you never would've met Allie and Danny." She pointed in the direction over her shoulder. "Never tasted my tea." She smiled good-naturedly. "God brought you here for a reason, Derrick. His ways are far above our ways."

"Yes, but I'm not sure He can condone what I've done, yet I didn't feel I had a choice."

"Wow, that's quite an introduction." Shannon lounged with her back against the chair like she had all day to listen, and he sensed no judgment from her.

"I originally came here on my younger sister's behalf. Her name was Sandy. She had cancer. When she knew she was dying, she confessed to me about her past—the extent of her drug use and that she'd given birth to a son."

Shannon's eyes grew wide. "Danny," she whispered.

Derrick nodded. "All Sandy had left of the memory of her son was a worn photo and a couple of names in Walla Walla that I could follow up on."

"Wow." Shannon rose to tend to the whistling kettle. "I wondered if it was my wild imagination." She poured tea into two mugs. "But you and Danny. . .it's not just your physical resemblance." She set the cups on the table and sat. "It's something intangible, like your passion for life and magnetic personalities."

Derrick smiled. "You should have met my sister."

"She must've loved having a big, protective brother like you. I'm an only child." She shrugged, then refocused on him. "Why didn't you come right out and tell Allie when you discovered Danny was your nephew? It wasn't like you'd come to town to steal him from the Vahns."

"I couldn't tell her. Sandy made me promise. She wanted me to check on Danny, make sure he was with a good family, and leave town without revealing her identity or mine. She didn't want to disturb his life in any way. We were worried about what my father would do if he discovered he had a grandson. Turns out our fears were well-grounded." He took a swallow of tea. "Anyway, everything was going well enough until I—"

"Started to fall in love with Allie?" Shannon pressed her

hand over her heart, and he would have laughed if not for the bitter ending.

"Yes, I started to fall in love with Allie. I also loved my nephew as though I'd known him all my life. And Betsy felt like a second mom to me. I didn't have that kind of warm upbringing." He sighed. "I was selfish for spending the time with them that I did. I should have gone home as soon as I saw Danny was fine."

"I understand why you did it." Shannon played with the handle of her mug. "So Sandy finally gave you permission to tell Allie?"

"Yes, right before she died."

Shannon sat back in the chair. "So you went to Allie after your sister's passing? Confessed everything? And she wouldn't forgive you?"

Derrick snorted a humorless laugh. "No, it gets much, much worse." He felt the pain anew and drew a breath. "My father found out about Danny."

Shannon's eyes widened. "Oh no. And he got to Allie first?"

"Exactly. He went to the Vahns' house and informed them the adoption was coerced. He demanded joint custody and threatened Allie and Betsy with a legal battle if they refused."

Shannon blew out a breath of air. "I know what Allie's reaction was. She came up angry, hurt, and fighting." She frowned. "Was it true? Was the adoption coerced?"

He nodded. "Yes, in a manner of speaking. By law the adoptive parents should have been investigated and approved. Sandy should have been given time to reconsider before signing papers. Instead she signed as soon as Danny was born, and he was whisked away."

"Man oh man. And Paige handled the adoption, right?"

Derrick nodded. "Keep in mind that my sister had no regrets. She was living on the street at the time and couldn't have cared for him. But she wanted to make sure he was okay. That's where I came in. I wanted her to go home with a peaceful heart."

Shannon frowned in thought. "Do you remember the story of Rahab in the Bible?"

That came out of left field. Derrick just nodded.

"How she hid the Israelite spies from the local authorities and got protection for her family?"

"Yes."

"Well, in a way, you were doing the same thing. You were hiding Danny from being hurt while you got information for your sister. You were protecting everyone. And you never outright lied." Shannon slapped her hands on the table. "We've got to straighten this out." She stood, went to the counter, and picked up her cell phone. "The Bible says if we know the truth, the truth will set us free."

"I don't see Allie ever trusting me again. She's been deceived too many times." Derrick's shoulders sagged with defeat. "But if you're willing to try."

Shannon tossed her phone on the counter. "I won't call. I'll close the store and go pay Allie a visit instead." She picked up a big ring of keys. "I hate cell phones. You may as well stick your head in the microwave."

"Um. . .I never thought of it that way." Derrick followed her outside.

She patted him on the shoulder. "Pray, Derrick." She whirled away to her truck.

Derrick headed for his vehicle. Did God answer those kinds of prayers? He had deceived the very people who'd treated him with nothing but kindness.

Allie's words came back to haunt him, *"I can't abide lying."*

twenty-three

Allie and Danny returned from the blackberry patch with two buckets of berries. She handed them to him. "Take these inside to Granny."

"Wow, I can't believe Mr. Derrick is my uncle," Danny said for at least the eighth time, his eyes filled with wonder as he headed inside.

Just great. Her nephew was still impressed with "the hero" and glad he was related by blood.

Allie's cell phone vibrated in its holder on her belt. She snatched it up. *Michael.* "Hello?"

"Allie." His voice sounded strained. "I just talked to Paige. She's hysterical. I want to verify what you told her." He repeated her conversation with his sister.

"That's right," Allie said. "And did she tell you about the payments Luke made to her?"

After a long pause, Michael cleared his throat. "Payments?"

Allie explained the check stubs she'd found. "She claims she was having an affair with Luke and he helped support her."

Silence from the other end. "Michael, are you there?"

"Yes—yes, I am." He cleared his throat again. "Listen, no matter what you think of me, please know I don't want your family hurt. I'm looking into this. And, Allie, you'd do well not to talk to any of the Owenses until you have legal representation. I had my doubts about Derrick all along. I'm here if you need me."

Of course Michael would use this opportunity to make himself look good, to get Allie back. As she hung up, she heard a vehicle approaching and walked to the front of the house. It was Shannon in her old green truck, tearing up the driveway like a maniac, spewing dust in every direction.

151

After she slid to a stop, she hopped from the truck. "We need to talk!"

"Yes, we do," Allie said. They exchanged hugs. "I'm so glad to see you. You'll never believe—"

"I already know." Shannon sank onto a porch step and patted the place next to her, suddenly composed and relaxed. "Let's sit. It's a lovely day."

Allie complied. "What do you mean?"

"The sun is shining and—"

"I'm not asking about the weather, Shannon! I'm asking how you know what happened to me. Are we on the same page here?"

Shannon folded her hands in her lap and nodded.

"You spoke with Derrick, didn't you?"

Shannon inhaled. "How cool that you picked up on that. Maybe you're getting more in tune with body language."

"I doubt it," Allie snapped. "Otherwise I would have picked up on Derrick's lies."

Shannon waved her hand in the air. "I was thinking about what deception really is."

Allie blinked. "What?"

"And then I thought about Luke and Michael. Especially Michael. Anyway, I'm not sure 'lie' is the right word to use for what Derrick did." Shannon's eyes were filled with compassion. A sure sign that Derrick had gotten to her.

"Derrick *did* lie."

"Did he?" Shannon twisted her thumb ring. "He never told you anything that wasn't true, did he? Did he purposefully set out to deceive you with malice in his heart?"

"What does that mean?" Allie gave an inpatient shrug. "This wound can't be healed with soothing words. I know you mean well, but I—"

"Okay, stop." Shannon held up her hand. "This is one time you're not going to cut me off. You're not going to stop listening like you do sometimes. It's too important to your life and Danny's."

Allie's breaths came fast and hard with irritation. "Go ahead then. I don't have all afternoon. I have to make calls and fill my schedule with more work to earn enough money to hire an attorney to keep the boy who already belongs to us." She felt the threat of tears all over again. "Did Derrick tell you that, too?"

"Yes." Shannon patted her back. "That's not what Derrick wants, Allie. And I believe him with my whole heart."

"Of course you would. You have an almost unnatural ability to see only the good in people. Like my mother. And speaking of liars, guess who called me?"

Shannon raised her brows. "This is the only conversational digression I'll allow you, then I get to talk."

"Okay." Allie told Shannon what Paige had said and then about Michael's call.

"Hmm. Trying to get on your good side." Shannon nodded. "I think God is at work here. I'm imagining a big creaky mill slowly turning. It might seem to take forever, but the grain is getting ground up."

Allie wasn't sure she could see it. Shannon was particularly confusing today. "Okay. . .God is working."

"So now it's my turn. Remember the story of Rahab in the Bible?"

"What?" Allie asked.

"When you hear why Derrick did what he did, maybe you'll open your heart enough to forgive him."

Allie sat back and closed her eyes, hoping it might help her understand. "All right. Spill it."

&

Derrick walked into his father's office late that night without bothering to knock. He sat at his large cherry desk and looked up.

"Why'd you do it, Dad? Why did you threaten the Vahns?"

"You know why." Dad stood and tossed a folder toward Derrick and pointed at it. "This is all the information I need to go to court. I'm not going to change my mind."

Derrick approached the desk, but ignored the file. "So if you win this court battle—and you won't—you'll do what? Force a nine-year-old who adores his adoptive family to love you?"

Dad's eyes glittered. "If they don't agree to shared custody, I will do whatever I have to."

Derrick fought the anger that burned inside him. "You might want to reconsider."

"Are you threatening me, son?" He dropped to the edge of the desk and crossed his arms. "Your very generous paycheck comes from Owens Realty. You'd do well to remember which side your bread is buttered on."

Money. Again. "You can keep your money." Derrick put his hands, palms down, on his father's desk. "You think money can buy anything, don't you?" *Even love,* he was tempted to add.

"All of a sudden you're the poor little rich boy, are you? Never heard you complain over the years when you squired your many women around town in expensive sports cars, spending money without a second thought." Dad drew a noisy breath, went behind his desk, and sat. "I've got work to do, if you don't mind."

"I do mind," Derrick said. "Why do you always play the womanizing card with me? You know I've changed."

"Hmm, that's right, you found religion," Dad said, a trace of laughter in his voice. "But I think we're more alike than you'd care to admit. Could be I've met my match."

Derrick shook his head. "I used to wish that. I tried to emulate you. But now the last person in the world I'd be like is you."

Dad's head snapped back as if Derrick had hit him.

"You're trying to intimidate and bully an innocent family. Danny is theirs, and that's exactly how Sandy wanted it. Danny's a happy kid, he's well cared for, and—"

"And nothing!" Dad shot out of his chair. "His adoptive parents are dead. He's being raised by a blacksmith and a cleaning woman when he could have all this." He waved his arms, then his brows drew together and he snorted. "What's that look on your face? If you and Sandy had come to me with this situation first, I could've handled things. You"—he pointed a shaking finger—"are the cause of all this confusion!"

"A situation? Is that how you refer to Sandy's son?"

"Ah, now you're talking sense. Danny is *Sandy's* son." Dad punched his right fist into his left hand. "*My* grandson. An Owens. Not an orphan meant to live on a dirt farm in the middle of nowhere. Left alone to break his arm." Looking satisfied with himself, Dad dropped into his leather armchair.

Derrick backed toward the door.

"Where are you going?"

"I'm leaving, Dad," Derrick said quietly. "I want out of the company, out of this family for good." At the slack-jawed look on his father's face, anger seeped from him replaced by great sadness.

"You're leaving us for them? You're going to walk out on us after we lost Sandy?" Dad came around to the other side of the desk and clamped his hands behind his back. "And your mother, what about her?"

"I'm leaving because I won't be a part of what you're doing. Mom will always be a part of my life—I'll be in touch with her regularly." He studied his father intently, but the man's face gave away nothing. "Mom doesn't know Danny exists, does she? She's got nothing to do with this idiotic threat."

"No, she doesn't. It would kill her to know Sandy's son is being raised by strangers."

"Hogwash!" Derrick's muscles went rigid, and he drew a breath and asked God to give him peace. "You don't know the Vahns. Allie and Betsy love Danny with all their hearts. Yeah, they have financial problems, but they work hard to give *your* grandson everything he needs." He had his father's full attention now, and Derrick took another breath lest he choke up. "You should've seen the birthday party Allie had for Danny. It must've cost her a week's pay."

Dad stared over Derrick's shoulder.

What was the use? His words were falling on deaf ears.

"I'd rather Danny be raised without all the things I had. You gave me plenty of material things, but I needed your heart. That's what Danny needs, too, and he's got that with Allie and Betsy." Derrick swiped his suit jacket off the back of the chair and headed for the door.

"So just like that, you're walking out?" Dad asked before he could read the message.

"I'll have everything out of the guest house by Monday. And if you pursue action against the Vahns, I will use everything in my power to help fight you." Derrick opened the door and stopped. Standing there in the hall was Mom, her face whiter than it had been, if that were possible. Tears wet her face.

"How long have you been here?" Derrick whispered.

twenty-four

On Monday morning Allie loaded her truck with supplies, then zipped her bag closed. She had one appointment with a normal horse, then she'd have to deal with Eddieboy again. Seems he had spent two days hock-deep in manure in his stall, and the thrush grew worse. Not that she should complain. Frank paid her well, and she was able to slip in the appointment between two others. But today she was going to lay down the law. No animal, no matter how cranky, deserved to be treated like that. Besides, dealing with Eddieboy would keep her mind off everything Shannon had told her about Derrick. Allie didn't know how she felt or what to think.

As she pulled down the driveway, a big blue Lincoln headed toward her. She got closer and recognized Philip Maynard. The mayor hailed her, waving his chunky hand out the window.

Allie pulled onto the side of the drive and waited. He stopped his car alongside her. "Allie, I need to speak with you."

Her first question was, "Why?" Lately every encounter with a Maynard spelled trouble. In fact it was her encounter with Philip at the parade that had led to her meeting Derrick. "What can I do for you?"

"Um, got some place we can sit?" He cut the engine and tugged at his shirt collar.

"Yeah, sure." Allie indicated the picnic bench near the house, a myriad of scenarios passing through her mind. Did he come in peace or to threaten them in some way?

After they settled at the table, the mayor smiled. "How's everybody doing? Everybody okay?"

"Philip, I know you didn't come here for small talk. Please just get on with it."

"Right." He nodded, and his smile disappeared. "I'm ashamed of my daughter."

Allie gasped. "Paige told you about the. . ." *Affair? Adoption? Money?* The words stuck in her throat.

"Paige confided in Michael, and he's the one who told me everything. You know, my son's got plenty of faults, but he's letter of the law when it comes to business."

Her mind raced. "Business? Luke gave Paige—"

"Close to fifty thousand dollars. I know." Philip sighed. "And I intend to give you back every red cent."

"Why?" As much as her family desperately needed the money, her suspicions grew. This show of humility from Philip Maynard was out of character to the extreme. "What did Michael tell you exactly?"

Philip's eyes narrowed. "Paige misled you." He pulled a hankie from his pocket and dabbed sweat from his brow. "When Cindy was a nurse in the rehab clinic in the Tri-Cities, she met Sandy Owens, Danny's biological mother."

"Yes, I know all this and that Paige handled the paperwork."

He breathed heavily and wiped his balding head, and she felt a pang of compassion for the man. Mayor Maynard looked her in the eye. "Did you ever ask yourself, 'Why Paige?'"

Allie nodded. "Yes. She said it was because she loved Luke. She also told me she was having an affair with him."

"That's not true, Allie. Your brother was a good man, completely blind to what was going on. He wasn't aware the adoption was questionable."

"If she didn't do it for Luke, then why? Paige would've never handled the adoption out of the goodness of her heart. Cindy and Paige disliked each other intensely."

"Paige didn't do it out of the 'goodness of her heart.' She used it as an ace in the hole to endear herself to Luke. She never did get over him."

"Endear herself how?" Her heart pounded in her ears, and she struggled for breath.

"Then Paige could come to him with the cold facts later,

in hopes that he'd leave Cindy for deceiving him. When that didn't work, Paige got angry and blackmailed your brother. If Luke didn't give her money, Paige threatened to expose Cindy, even at the expense of losing her law license." He wagged his head. "I don't know where I went wrong with my daughter. Gave her everything till she took advantage and I cut her off."

That explained all the fights Luke and Cindy had. Cindy's bitterness toward Paige. As Allie digested the information, she took pity on the mayor. Tears rushed to her eyes. "I'm so relieved to know my brother wasn't cheating on his wife. It was killing me to think Luke was a fraud."

"No, Luke was only protecting his wife and Danny. He hid things from you, but that's what a good man does—anything to protect family."

Just like Derrick had been protecting his sister. What Luke had done to protect Cindy—who wasn't dying—Derrick had done for his sister, only in a different way. He'd even tried to protect Danny, her, and Ma. In her mind's eye, she saw him sitting on the bale of straw, trying to get her to understand, but she'd refused.

"Why did you tell me all this?"

"Yes, well," Philip said with a wave of his hand. "Don't mistake me for being altruistic. I'm protecting my own family. If I didn't tell you, Michael would have. He wants to get back into your good graces. Besides, from what I understand, the Owenses might try to sue for custody. All this might play out in court, and I'm not going to risk my reputation for what my daughter did."

"That's why you're offering me the money?"

"Well, if you take recompense and don't press charges against Paige, the DA, who is a friend of mine, won't take this to court, and we'll avoid a public scandal. Unless Owens raises a huge stink, which I hope he doesn't. But Paige's future remains to be seen. She may lose her license to practice law."

"I don't want a scandal either, and I don't want to see Paige behind bars, but I might need that money for legal fees to fight the Owenses."

Philip swung his heavily jowled head from side to side. "Try to settle out of court. Take it from an old man. Maybe you could see it in your heart to let the kid see his grandparents. I know how I'd feel if I knew I had a grandson somewhere."

He struggled to his feet, and Allie followed him to his car. "Again, I'm sorry for what my daughter did, Allie. And the part Cindy played in all this."

Cindy. Paige. The Owenses. Philip's words rang in her mind as he drove off. She walked toward the house feeling lighter. They wouldn't have to sell their property. They would be able to battle the Owenses if they chose to fight. Despite all the bad that had happened, she could tell her mother Luke was innocent of wrongdoing. Ma would want to pray together to thank God, and for the first time in a very long time, Allie was eager to join her with a grateful heart.

❧

The full weight of what he'd done hit Derrick as he glanced around the empty guest house. Along with moving his belongings to a small apartment, he'd talked to his financial advisor. Though he had money of his own, walking away from his family meant he would no longer live a privileged life. Oddly enough, that idea challenged him and gave him the strength to follow through with his painful decision.

"So you finally stood up to the old man," Hank's voice came from behind him.

Derrick turned and saw him in the doorway. "Yes, I guess I did."

Hank dropped into a leather chair in the corner. "I'm not surprised. It was inevitable. I saw it, even when you were a kid. No need to wonder where you and Sandy got your willful streaks."

"Yeah, right. Maybe the showdown was inevitable, but not what I wanted." He zipped his suitcases closed. "Promise me you'll look after Mom?"

"You got it, but I think you'll discover your mother has a backbone of steel. She might have appeared vulnerable and acquiescent all these years, and especially the last few weeks, but believe me, the woman knows how to run the show."

"I hope so," Derrick said.

"Let me help you carry those to your truck."

The two men walked in silence out the door to the driveway.

"Will you fight for her?" Hank asked.

"What?" Derrick stacked the suitcases in the back of the Silverado.

"That young lady you like so much. . .Allie. Seems to me she might be worth fighting for."

Derrick shrugged. "She hasn't called me. Danny has, but nothing from Allie. I can't go back to Walla Walla on just my nephew's invitation. I need her permission."

"She won't call you. From what you've told me, Allie doesn't seem that sort." Hank slapped him on the back. "If I were you, I'd go see her. Tell her what you've done in the name of love."

&

Derrick stopped at a light and pondered Hank's words. How about a happy medium? He'd call Shannon, get her opinion. By now she had spoken to Allie, and she'd know whether or not a visit from him would disturb the Vahns.

He dialed.

"The Quaint Shop, good afternoon."

"Shannon, it's Derrick." He infused his voice with cheer he didn't feel.

"Derrick! I was going to call you, but my pastor's wife pulled me aside after our prayer meeting."

She paused, and he heard murmuring in the background. "Shannon, you there?"

"Yes, sorry, a customer asked a question. Anyway, Portia, that's Pastor's wife, told me that I give out too much un-solicited advice. How embarrassing. Portia said she knows I mean well, but I have to allow God to do the work."

"Um, let's back up a sec. What does that have to do with me?" Derrick took an exit onto the highway toward Walla Walla. Is that where he wanted to go?

"If I keep talking right now, I'll end up giving you my advice."

"Shannon? I'm the one who asked you to speak with Allie. Therefore your advice wouldn't be unsolicited." He went on to tell her what had transpired with his father. "I want to tell Allie that I'm going to help them fight if they have to."

Another long silence. "Shannon?"

"Yes. I'm thinking."

Shannon was nice, but one of the most confusing people he'd ever talked to. "I'm on my way to Walla Walla, but I'm wondering if I should turn around and head home. I don't want to upset Allie or Betsy. If there's a chance that I'll make things even worse by going over there, I don't want to come."

"I've decided I'll tell you exactly what I think. You must come. Allie has some appointments. Call me when you get into town, and I'll confirm where she is and give you directions. I don't think you'll make things worse." There was a smile in Shannon's voice, and a tiny flicker of hope came alive inside him.

twenty-five

"Stop that!" Allie ducked to avoid Eddieboy's third attempt to chomp her arm as she walked past his head.

He snorted.

"Yeah, yeah, whatever. Carnivore." She checked his hoof one more time. "Frank needs a serious talking to. If this keeps up, your foot is going to rot away." For some reason she felt sorry for the little pony, despite his rotten disposition. If he'd been better cared for, he'd have half a chance to bloom.

The barn door squeaked open. "Frank!" Allie yelled. "You and I need a word. I know Eddieboy is cranky. So are you, but you can't allow him to continue this way."

She heard footsteps, but no response. "Do you want me to call the ASPCA?"

Allie put the pony's foot down and stood to face Frank. "Oh no," she whispered and ducked quickly behind Eddieboy's neck. "It's Derrick. I don't know what to say to him after all this." She smoothed back her hair. After any encounter with Eddieboy, she looked like a tornado victim.

Derrick glanced around, noticed her peering at him over the pony's mane, and held up his hand. "Don't run away," he said softly.

She straightened and lifted her chin. "What are you doing here?"

"Looking for you." He took several steps toward her.

"How did you find me?"

"Shannon told me you'd be here."

Why had she bothered to ask? Shannon had just called her twenty minutes ago to ask her if she wanted to go out to dinner. The traitor. "What do you want?" Allie sounded rude, but she still wasn't sure how she felt about anything right now. She was too numb. "Did you come here to try to sweet-talk me?"

"No." He moved toward her again and stopped a couple of feet away. "I'm here to tell you I'm on your side. I'll hire a lawyer myself if my father insists on this ridiculous fight."

Of all the things he could have said, that wasn't what she expected. "What exactly do you mean?"

Derrick shoved his hands in his jean pockets. "I told my father I won't be working for him anymore. And I won't be living on his property." He shrugged. "I guess I disowned myself."

Eddieboy took another swipe at her, and she shoved his nose away. "You walked away from your family?"

"I did. I don't expect you to let me back into your life, but I want you to know that I'll do whatever it takes to see that Danny stays with you and your mother."

Allie stared, struggling to process his words. "You disowned yourself?"

"Yes." Derrick took a deep breath. "I'll call you if I hear anything. If you hear anything, get served with papers, or whatever, you call me, okay?"

She let his words sink in. "Yes, fine." Derrick hadn't tried to charm her like Michael always had.

He took his hands from his pockets and extended them toward her, but suddenly dropped them to his side. "Please hug Danny for me?" he asked as he backed away.

She nodded. Her mind was computing very slowly. "Right. Sure. Will do." *He came to tell me this in person when he could have called.* That took courage.

"I've got one more stop to make," he said. "I need to tell your mother the same thing. I owe it to her."

"She's at Shannon's shop," Allie volunteered. "Danny's at the sitter's." Now he risked Ma's cold shoulder.

"Right. She's working then."

She nodded like her head was on a spring.

He opened his mouth and snapped it shut. After a moment's

hesitation, he turned and walked from the barn.

Allie watched the door shut. Derrick had walked away from his family because he cared enough to fight so that Danny could stay with her and Ma. Did someone who wasn't trustworthy do something like that? The Bible said there was no greater love than if a man laid down his life for his friend.

"Derrick?" Allie whispered, willing her feet to move.

The slam of his vehicle door met her ears.

"Derrick!" she yelled. Eddieboy jumped. "Oh, get over yourself," she told the pony. She left him tied in the barn aisle and ran outside.

"Derrick, wait!" As she watched the retreating taillights, she jumped up and down, waving her hands in the air to get his attention, but he didn't see her.

༄

Derrick felt his cell phone vibrating on his belt, but couldn't bring himself to answer. Right now it was best he didn't speak to anybody. He needed a few minutes. The hope he'd had for reconciliation with Allie had died. He hadn't been able to find the words to ask her forgiveness, perhaps because he didn't feel deserving.

He drove toward Shannon's shop as quickly as the speed limit would allow, prepared to tell Betsy everything. Get it all out, then leave the Vahns alone.

Lord, I want to do the right thing, no matter what the cost.

He parked, then walked toward The Quaint Shop, dreading the look of disappointment on Betsy's face when she saw him.

As he pulled open the door, he lingered at the front of the store for a moment, but the cowbell had alerted Shannon and Betsy to his presence. They turned, and both greeted him with bright smiles. Why?

Moving toward them slowly, Derrick tilted his head. "Good afternoon, ladies."

"I already told Betsy everything," Shannon blurted out. "Figured it would save you time."

Betsy came from behind the counter and hurried over to him. "Did you talk to Allie yet?"

"Well, I tried." Derrick shrugged.

"And?" Shannon clasped her hands like she anticipated good news.

"Allie was dealing with that scraggly pony." No. Truth was she used the creature as a diversion. "She didn't say much."

Shannon and Betsy exchanged glances.

"I'm going to call her." Shannon turned, then searched under the mess on her counter. "Where's that stupid phone?"

Much as she meant well, he couldn't expect Shannon to run interference for him. "No, don't call her."

Betsy and Shannon stared at him, eyes round with sympathy.

"It's okay, really." He backed away. "Allie has to make decisions for herself."

The front door banged open with a crash. Shannon and Betsy's eyes widened, and Derrick turned.

Allie stood in the doorway.

"I have something to say." She stared at him, her auburn hair as wild as the day he'd dragged her from Chester's back.

His breath caught in his lungs. The silence that followed was deafening.

She took a step toward him. "Derrick."

He couldn't decode the look on her beautiful face. "Yes?"

Allie ran at him and flung her arms around his neck. "Derrick," she whispered into his shoulder.

He held her close and swung her around in a circle. When he finally put her down, he gently kissed her cheek.

She backed up. "I know what you did was for your sister's sake." She clutched the lapels of his shirt. "You never meant to hurt anyone. You were trying to protect everyone, including my family."

"I would never hurt you on purpose. Never," he whispered into her hair. "I want to love you for the rest of my life." He kissed her soundly.

The sound of applause came from behind him, followed by

a whistle. Derrick lifted his head and laughed. "I forgot we had an audience."

Allie peered around Derrick and winked at her mother and Shannon, then looked back into his eyes, smiling.

Derrick's cell phone vibrated again, and he decided he'd better pick up this time.

"That better be important." Allie kissed him before joining the other two women at the counter.

He glanced at the screen and was hit with a pang of worry. "It's my mom." She rarely called, and when she did, it wasn't good news.

"Hey, Mom. What's up? Something wrong?"

"Not a thing." Her voice was cool, as if she'd returned to the woman she'd been before Sandy died. "I know about Danny. I know what your father has tried to do. I want you to go to Danny's family and tell them they will have no further trouble from us."

Stunned silent, he waited for more.

"I love your father, but I've learned over the years the only way to deal with him is to let him experience the consequences of his actions. After you left, I told him I would move into a hotel if he insisted on threatening the Vahn family. We want to see Danny, of course, but I will appeal to Allie and her mother myself. The Vahns need no longer fear legal recourse."

"Mom, thank you." Derrick smiled. "I'm right here with them."

Allie, Shannon, and Betsy stared at him.

"Pass on the message. I'll deal with your father." She paused. "And I think it's time you tell that young woman how you really feel."

"How did you know?"

"I know you confide in Hank. I cornered him in the kitchen and threatened to dent his pots and pans."

Derrick laughed. "So Hank caved."

"Of course he did. You know how he loves his cookware. Now, dear. You call me soon. Let me know how things are going with your young lady. And tell Betsy and Allie the next Owens they talk to besides you will be me. Ask them. . ." She paused. "Ask them to please consider allowing me to see my grandson."

epilogue

Allie stood at her vanity mirror and adjusted her pearl necklace.

"Allie, you look beautiful beyond words." Shannon joined her at the window and fussed with her bridal veil. "A princess, that's what you look like."

Tears filled Allie's eyes, and she fanned her face. "Don't make me cry. I don't know how to redo my makeup like that professional artist."

"Okay, I won't." Shannon laughed and hugged her. "I've imagined my own wedding day, but never dreamt of anything this lovely." She stepped back and sighed. "Wait till Derrick sees you."

"Derrick." Allie smiled. "At the mention of his name, my heart pounds harder than the first time we met."

Hands clasped to her heart, Shannon exhaled heavily. "Oh how romantic."

"Tell me I'm not dreaming."

"You're not."

Allie reached out and smoothed the satin collar of Shannon's lavender dress. "You're so special. No girl could ask for a better friend or maid of honor."

"Now *I'm* going to cry. . .again." Shannon grabbed a tissue and dabbed at her eyes. "I hardly ever wear makeup. Talk about not knowing how to fix my face."

Allie grabbed her hand and walked her to the mirror. "This is how you should dress all the time. You're too gorgeous to hide under baggy clothes."

Shannon tilted her head and smoothed her hands down the sides of her gown. "Only under duress." She shot Allie a telling look, and they both laughed. "I can't see myself changing my style, but if it'll catch me a winner like Derrick, maybe I would."

"God's got someone extra special for you, too." Allie flounced to the window and looked out. "People are filling the chairs."

Shannon came to her side. "So they are. Look at your mom and Mrs. Owens. They're like best friends already."

"Mrs. Owens said Sandy was responsible for all this." Allie's eyes blurred. "She said, 'Death brings rebirth.'"

❧

On the back porch of Allie's house, Derrick glanced at the flower-adorned gazebo where he and Allie would be married. Danny stood next to him in a black tux much like Derrick's.

"You nervous, Uncle Derrick?"

"You betcha. Have you got the rings?" Derrick stepped back and scanned his nephew. "You're one handsome kid."

"Grandma Owens says I look like you." Danny appraised himself in the mirror. "That's probably good because you got Aunt Allie to marry you. It means you're handsome."

Derrick laughed. "Hey, you're right. I'm the one who got the best of the deal. Now check your pocket again for the rings."

"I got 'em."

"Okay then, are we ready?" Derrick felt his heart pounding through his shirt. He swallowed past the lump in his throat and put his hand on Danny's shoulder. "Did I ever tell you you're my hero?"

Danny stared up at him, frowning. "What do you mean? What did I do?"

"You always believed in me, and that's one of the best things a hero can do for someone. It gave me the courage to face your Aunt Allie."

"I'm only a kid," Danny said, "but even I knew you liked her. You were always staring at her."

"I know," Derrick headed for the gazebo. "She might've stared at me a couple of times, too, you know."

"Yeah, maybe," Danny conceded and walked tall beside Derrick, passing family and friends that had come to celebrate with them.

Derrick sent up a silent prayer of gratitude to God for restoring his family, for Allie, and for giving Allie and him the greatest kid on earth. And he thanked God for his sister. She would be so proud today.

He stood with the pastor beside the gazebo, Danny at his side. The wedding march commenced, and he set his sights to the back door of the house. Allie emerged with Derrick's dad, their arms looped. His father's chest was puffed out with pride. He was growing to love Allie like a daughter.

She looked like a princess in a white satin ball gown. Tears rose in his eyes as she walked toward him, smiling.

His mom and Betsy held on to each other. They'd foregone the traditional bride and groom sides and stood side by side.

After Allie reached him, Derrick took her hands in his, and they faced one another, repeating their vows after the minister.

"To love, honor, and cherish. . .as long as we both shall live."

"You may now kiss your beautiful bride."

He lifted the veil, leaned down, and kissed her soundly on her welcoming lips. When he was done, the attendees cheered.

"Derrick?" Allie whispered in his ear.

"Yes?"

"You are the hero of my heart."

Author's Note

Our setting, Walla Walla, is a beautiful town near the border of Washington and Oregon. We've tried to be as accurate as possible when we've written about real places in the town, but like most authors, we've taken some literary license.

What's real: Bright's Candies is a real store. The Marcus Whitman Hotel is also a real place. Frog Hollow Road exists, as do the Blue Mountains. And every year there is an onion festival.

What's not real: Philip Maynard is not the mayor of Walla Walla. (In fact, any resemblance between any of our characters and anyone in Walla Walla is totally accidental.) The Vahn farm is a total work of fiction, as is The Quaint Shop. To our knowledge, there never has been an onion parade.

A Letter To Our Readers

Dear Reader:
In order that we might better contribute to your reading enjoyment, we would appreciate your taking a few minutes to respond to the following questions. We welcome your comments and read each form and letter we receive. When completed, please return to the following:

Fiction Editor
Heartsong Presents
PO Box 719
Uhrichsville, Ohio 44683

1. Did you enjoy reading *A Hero for Her Heart* by Candice Speare and Nancy Toback?
   ❏ Very much! I would like to see more books by this author!
   ❏ Moderately. I would have enjoyed it more if

   _____

   _____

   _____

2. Are you a member of **Heartsong Presents**? ❏ Yes ❏ No
   If no, where did you purchase this book? _____

   _____

3. How would you rate, on a scale from 1 (poor) to 5 (superior), the cover design? _____

4. On a scale from 1 (poor) to 10 (superior), please rate the following elements.

   ____ Heroine   ____ Plot
   ____ Hero   ____ Inspirational theme
   ____ Setting   ____ Secondary characters

5. These characters were special because? _____

_____

_____

6. How has this book inspired your life? _____

_____

_____

7. What settings would you like to see covered in future
   Heartsong Presents books? _____

_____

_____

8. What are some inspirational themes you would like to see
   treated in future books? _____

_____

_____

9. Would you be interested in reading other **Heartsong
   Presents** titles? ❏ Yes ❏ No

10. Please check your age range:
    ❏ Under 18   ❏ 18-24
    ❏ 25-34   ❏ 35-45
    ❏ 46-55   ❏ Over 55

Name _____

Occupation _____

Address _____

City, State, Zip_____

E-mail _____

COLORADO CRIMES

3 stories in 1

Pricilla Crumb's guest list has just turned into a suspect list. . .for murder. In this collection of three fun Rocky Mountain mysteries, Chef Pricilla Crumb dishes up trouble when she leaves her kitchen, hot on a murderer's trail.

Suspense, paperback, 448 pages, 5⅜" x 8"

Please send me ____ copies of *Colorado Crimes*. I am enclosing $7.97 for each.
(Please add $4.00 to cover postage and handling per order. OH add 7% tax.
If outside the U.S. please call 740-922-7280 for shipping charges.)

Name _____

Address _____

City, State, Zip _____

To place a credit card order, call 1-740-922-7280.
Send to: Heartsong Presents Readers' Service, PO Box 721, Uhrichsville, OH 44683

♡

HEARTSONG
P R E S E N T S

If you love Christian romance…

$10.⁹⁹

You'll love Heartsong Presents' inspiring and faith-filled romances by today's very best Christian authors…Wanda E. Brunstetter, Mary Connealy, Susan Page Davis, Cathy Marie Hake, and Joyce Livingston, to mention a few!

When you join Heartsong Presents, you'll enjoy four brand-new, mass-market, 176-page books—two contemporary and two historical—that will build you up in your faith when you discover God's role in every relationship you read about!

Imagine…four new romances every four weeks—with men and women like you who long to meet the one God has chosen as the love of their lives…all for the low price of $10.99 postpaid.

To join, simply visit www.heartsong presents.com or complete the coupon below and mail it to the address provided.

Mass Market 176 Pages

✂- -

YES! Sign me up for Heartsong!

NEW MEMBERSHIPS WILL BE SHIPPED IMMEDIATELY!
Send no money now. We'll bill you only $10.99 postpaid with your first shipment of four books. Or for faster action, call 1-740-922-7280.

NAME_____

ADDRESS_____

CITY_____ STATE _____ ZIP _____

MAIL TO: HEARTSONG PRESENTS, P.O. Box 721, Uhrichsville, Ohio 44683
or sign up at WWW.HEARTSONGPRESENTS.COM